The Inquisitor's Secretary

A Story from the Days of the Reformation
in the Netherlands

(1556-1566)

by W. J. D. van Dijck

NETHERLANDS REFORMED BOOK AND PUBLISHING
Grand Rapids, MI 49525

Translated from the Dutch by Cornelius Lambregste
with special permission from the publisher,
G.F. Callenbach, Nijkerk, Holland.

3rd Printing 2003

Copyright © 1993
Netherlands Reformed Book and Publishing Committee
Printed in the United States of America

Contents

1. The Fugitive 3
2. An Unexpected Hiding Place 10
3. What Harm Hiddesz Related 20
4. A Remarkable Sermon 33
5. The Heretic Hunt 37
6. The Clerk of the Inquisitor 48
7. A Surprising Discovery 55
8. The Escape 63
9. How Harm Hiddesz Was Saved 68
10. A Blessed Deathbed 73
11. An Important Dinner Conversation 85
12. Mounting Doubts 94
13. At Duivenvoorde Castle 101
14. In "The Stone" at Leyden 110
15. In the Cell and Before the Bailiff 120
16. The Recognition 142
17. Ten Years Later 152

1

The Fugitive

"Come on, Adriaan, don't give up, son! I already see the towers of Leyden over yonder. If we hurry, then in another half hour we shall be in the home of good friends where you can rest up by the warm hearth."

The man who spoke these words to the twelve-year-old boy walking beside him was tall and broad-shouldered. He stooped slightly under the weight of a black leather satchel which was tied on his back with a wide strap. Judging by his clothing, he was neither a peasant nor a burgher. Whenever the cold north wind blew up a flap of his large cloth mantle, it revealed that his jerkin and short pants were made of fine Delft cloth, which was worn by burghers only, whereas his crude shoes, tied with straps, resembled those of a peasant. A soft felt hat covered for a large part his bearded face.

The boy's clothing was exactly like that of the man except that instead of a broad-rimmed hat the boy wore a fur cap, the flaps of which protected his ears from the bitter cold.

Both walked along slowly and with difficulty. The path alongside the Vliet River, which was meant for towing-horses rather than for pedestrians, was frozen hard, and the big, rock-like clods made walking very difficult. The silence of the fast-approaching night was broken only by the monotonous scratching some farmer made with his skates on the solid ice floor while hurrying home, or by the croaking of some crows flying toward the wooded Hague Road. Suddenly the boy stood still and put his hand to his forehead.

The man, too, stood still and asked sympathetically, "What is the matter, son, can't you keep it up anymore? No wonder," he continued to himself, "he has been on his feet since early this morning, on impassable roads and in this cold."

"Oh Father," said the lad, whose name was Adriaan as we have heard, "the cold does not bother me. Just feel how hot my head is, and my knees are knocking together; oh Father, I can go no more. Honestly, I can't anymore!"

If at that moment the man had not supported the lad with his strong arm, the boy would have fallen down. The man became frightened. "Adriaan!" he cried, and his voice betrayed how alarmed he was; "my child, my dear child!" and bending one knee on the hard ground he laid the lad against his chest. The boy had shut his eyes.

"The cold must have gotten him," muttered the man, and holding his son with one hand, he got a small bottle from underneath his mantle with the other.

"Here, son," he said, "a drop of sweet wine will do you good."

After a few minutes the boy opened his eyes again and looked around, puzzled.

"Ah! you are feeling better now, aren't you?" asked the man. Adriaan's body was shaking all over and his teeth were chattering. He answered, "Yes, Father, but it is so strange. My legs feel like lead; I just can't walk."

"Well, just try it, slowly. Over there I see a farmhouse, near that little bridge. We shall go inside for a few minutes and after you have been in a warm room for a while and have rested up a bit, we shall go on. As you know, tomorrow is Christmas and I should like, also for your sake, to get to Folkert the tanner this evening yet."

The man then took his son's arm in his and soon they were in front of the gate that gave entrance to the farmyard. At his call, which was answered by the loud barking of a watchdog, there appeared a peasant who carried a lantern because, even though it could not be much later than about five o'clock, darkness had already set in.

"What do you want?" he asked, and his voice sounded anything but friendly.

"Good friend," the man said, "will you be so kind as to ask your master if we may come in for a few minutes? This lad is very tired, and chilled to the bone. I will gladly pay whatever expenses there are."

"I am the master myself," was the gruff answer. "And as far as paying is concerned, we know all about that. My house is no inn that is open to all kinds of beggars. If you have money on you, then move on to the ferryhouse; there you can get what you want."

"But you see," continued the man who was still supporting the boy, "that the lad can't move anymore. I beg of you, please let us sit by the fire for only half an hour."

"Over there is the ferryhouse," was the harsh reply, and the man pointed in the direction of Leyden; "and now get out of here." He then turned around, grumbling, walked to the doghouse, and unchained the watchdog. Barking loudly the mean creature stormed toward the gate.

"Come, my child," said the man as if it did not surprise him to be treated like that.

Both father and son continued their walk in silence.

"At least that grumpy farmer did not tell a lie because I see a light over there and the ferryboat frozen tight in the ice."

After a few minutes they reached the ferryhouse, a big brick building with windows that were half closed with shutters. The light inside shone through the little horn windowpanes above the shutters.

For a moment the man hesitated to lift the latch of the door, but one look at the tired, staggering boy was enough to remove all hesitancy. So he and his son entered the ferryman's waiting room.

It was a rather large room with a low ceiling; the heavy oak beams of which, nearly black from smoke and old age, bespoke strength rather than beauty. Around a big hearth-fire that was fed by heavy logs and chunks of dried peat sat a few peasants who were playing a game of cards in the sparse light of a couple of smoking candles. On the protruding part of the iron hearth-plate stood a few large pewter mugs filled with brown Delft beer that was as heady as it was famous.

"Good evening, everybody!" greeted the man. At this usual greeting everyone in the room turned around and looked, surprised and without answering, at the two who had entered.

The ferryman, however, a small but strongly built cross-eyed man, walked immediately over to the visitor who, still holding the boy by the hand, stood in the middle of the room.

"Good evening, sir," the ferryman said, and with more politeness than grace lifted the fur cap from his head to greet the new arrivals. The ferryman, commonly known as "cross-eyed Krijn," looked surprised, too. It was unusual at this time of the year to see strangers in his ferryhouse, as only farmers who lived along the Vliet and around Voorschoten and the Leyden Dam stopped in occasionally for a mug of warm beer.

"What can I do for you, sir?" the ferryman asked while he looked the stranger over from head to foot.

"We should like to rest up a bit, ferryman, and have a pint of warm beer. It's cold outside, and we are still a long way from Leyden," the stranger replied while he placed his son on

The Fugitive

one of the few benches in the corner and his satchel under the only low wooden table in the room.

"To Leyden, my friend, at this late hour?" cross-eyed Krijn exclaimed, with a look of amazement at the man. "But why on earth do you take the path along the Vliet? Isn't the main road better and easier to travel than the towing-path?"

"A strange bird!" mumbled one of the peasants who, cards in hand, had turned around and kept on staring at the visitors. "What do you say, Kees?"

"I don't care what he is; just pass the cards around!"

The two peasants continued their game.

"Indeed," the stranger now replied, "the path is not easy, but when a person is on the road for business, he can't be particular and, in any case, from the Dam it's the shortest way."

"That it is," agreed the ferryman, meanwhile placing the steaming beer before his guests. "But you realize that the gate is closed at seven o'clock?"

"Yes, I know, but I don't exactly have to be inside the city wall. I am expected by one of my friends outside the wall."

"I suppose that is at Krelis the vegetable grower's?" asked the curious ferryman.

The stranger did not reply. He had focused all his attention on his son who had put his head against his father's chest and could not be moved to drink the warm beer.

"Oh, it pounds so here," the lad groaned, holding his hand against his forehead.

"Poor boy," sighed the father, looking around undecidedly. He knew well enough that all the lad needed was a good bed and a few hours of rest.

Right then the latch of the front door was lifted again and a farmer holding a pair of skates in his hand, dressed in a short jerkin and wide short pants and a heavy scarf tied loosely around his neck, entered the room.

"Hello there, Krijn, where are you? Get me something warm to drink right away! It sure is cold out, Krelis!"

The card-playing Krelis accepted the offered hand rather hesitantly, which the farmer did not seem to notice. "Well, Teun, you there, too? And always playing cards, eh? Well, boy, this is really no time to wreck your brains over a game. Right now a fellow needs them all to figure out how to get his rent together. Christmas week, fellows, is a bad one for the farmer, for the landlord is not easy, and woe to the tenant who during this week does not show up with his shiny talers!"

"On your way home?" Krijn asked, placing a mug of beer before the farmer who had just arrived.

"Just went to the Dam a minute," the latter replied, and between two swallows of the warm beer he continued, "with the sleigh. Beautiful ice; but bitter cold, straight against the wind."

The farmer put down the mug on the iron plate in front of him, and then seemed to notice the stranger with the boy for the first time. For a second he looked very closely at the man, and it seemed as if a slight twitching in his face betrayed an inner emotion. But soon he had mastered himself.

Suddenly he got up, strode towards the stranger, and exclaimed in surprise; "Why Harmen, Harmen, is that you? What brought you here, man?" And while he extended his right hand to the stranger before him, he placed for only a second the index finger of his left hand on his mouth and said in a quick whisper, "Good friend, Harm Hiddesz!"

The stranger, whom the farmer had addressed as "Harmen" but whose name apparently was Harm Hiddesz, was startled. Even though his name had been whispered, here was someone whom he could not remember ever having seen, but who nevertheless knew him, and this the stranger seemed to fear the most.

The round, open face of the farmer put him somewhat at ease, however, and he shook the extended hand as though they were friends who had not seen each other for years.

The farmer sat down across from the man whom he had called Harm Hiddesz. "Where are you headed for?" he asked in a whisper.

"To Leyden," was the equally softly spoken answer.

"To Folkert?"

A nod was the affirmative answer.

"Impossible," the farmer replied. "Folkert has been seized from his bed last night. The trap has been set and I thank God that I can warn you not to run into it. But we must get on our way, and that right now. Outside we'll talk some more."

"Well, well, are you two getting acquainted?" the ever inquisitive ferryman asked, approaching the two men.

"Why, Krijn, wouldn't you be happy, too, to shake hands with an old acquaintance whom you hadn't seen for years? Have you never met Harmen? No? He's a jewel of a merchant, the kind you do not often meet in Holland. When I still lived by the Zijl, he visited us on the farm at least once every two weeks!"

"But, come on, Harmen," the talkative, noisy farmer continued; "if you still want to make it to Leyden, you had better hurry. Just put the boy in the sleigh and you sit beside him. Within another five minutes we will be quite a ways on our way!"

A few minutes later the sleigh, pushed by the farmer on skates, slid across the ice, while the lad slumbered uneasily underneath the mantle in the arms of his father.

2

An Unexpected Hiding Place

For more than ten minutes the sleigh, pushed by powerful arms, slid almost noiselessly across the solid ice floor that covered the Vliet. Then the farmer abruptly turned right. The stranger in the sleigh, whom from now on we shall call by his true name, Harm Hiddesz, seemed to awaken from deep thoughts.

"This is not the way to Leyden, is it?" he said, turning around to the farmer.

"Certainly not," the man answered; "I told you before that it isn't safe for you there!"

"But who are you, seeing you know me while I don't remember ever having seen you, and where are you taking us?"

"I am taking you to a place where right now it is still safe; there we shall talk further."

And again the sleigh sped on while the farmer's skates scratched across the ice.

With a short turn he suddenly stopped in front of a farmhouse that was hidden behind a cluster of trees and short, dense brush.

"Is that your house?" Harm Hiddesz asked.

"No," the farmer said. "I am going inside for a few minutes and will be right back. Just take it easy for the moment."

At the loud barking of the farm dog there appeared a short fellow whom we must describe in some detail, as we shall meet him more often in the course of our story. We called him a little fellow because he was, as far as his size was concerned, far below average and his short stature contrasted greatly with that of the big farmer. His head seemed to have sunk between his shoulders and his long arms dangled beside his body like the handle of a pump. In the darkness his face was not clearly distinguishable. His voice was heavy and jerky as of one who speaks with great difficulty.

The farmer, who had nimbly jumped onto the shore, exchanged a few words with him and both went into the house, leaving Harm Hiddesz and his son behind.

Harm Hiddesz looked around, searchingly; then, lifting his eyes to the heavens in which now thousands of stars glittered, he said softly, "Faithful heavenly Father, art Thou carrying me into the bosom of unknown friends, or hast Thou prepared new afflictions for me? Thou knowest, Lord, that Thy servant desires to walk willingly in the way where Thou wilt lead him, even though this way may take him through deep places. But for the sake of Thy dear Son, Lord, look down in mercy upon the lad whose strength is not sufficient to follow me in the work that Thou hast called me to perform!"

Just then the farmer, followed by the short little fellow and someone else, came outside.

"Come on, Harm, my sister has already cleared a good place for you by the hearth. You carry the boy and I'll take care of the luggage."

Harm Hiddesz took the boy, who was still sleeping, in his arms and followed the second farmer who went ahead of him into the house.

The little fellow pulled the sleigh upon the shore and shoved it near the door of the house.

Harm had to stoop when entering the low door opening of the otherwise rather high and sizable farmhouse. Going through the front room, where the cooling trough stood and where cleanly scoured copperware was lined up against the wall, he entered a large room with a low ceiling and a floor of hardened clay. The room was sparsely illuminated by a few tallow candles. Already at the threshold he was heartily welcomed by the lady of the house.

"Be welcome in my house, dear sir, and may Christmas Eve be blessed unto you!"

Harm Hiddesz was surprised at the words of this greeting which were unusual for a lowly farmer's wife.

"But what are you carrying there," she continued, "a child?"

"Dear woman, my little son fell asleep from tiredness and I fear that he is not well. I should very much like to lay him down somewhere, even if it were in some corner of the warm stable."

"In the stable!" the woman said and she clapped her hands together. "The son of Harm in the stable! Never! Just follow me; I'll show the way." She took one of the candles in her hand and led Harm to a little alcove where he laid Adriaan down in a nice clean bed.

The lad opened his eyes while his father was taking off his outer clothes; but, seemingly used to it, he showed not the least surprise to be in a strange environment.

"Oh, I'm comfortable here," he said; "but ah, how my head pounds, and I'm so thirsty."

Sympathetically the farmer's wife put her hand on his forehead. "The little fellow has a fever," she said. She quickly wet a cloth and tied it around his burning head. Then she gave him a drink of water.

"Father, I have to pray yet!"

The father bent his knees before the lad's bed and Adriaan said the following little prayer:

> *Praise, honor, and thanksgiving be*
> *To God the heavenly Father eternally,*
> *Who through Jesus has delivered us*
> *And who daily gives food and clothes to us;*
> *To God, the all-wise and only King, be*
> *Praise and honor from eternity to eternity. Amen.*

A little while afterwards Harm Hiddesz was sitting in the small circle of friends in whose midst he had so unexpectedly been received.

While the farmer's wife was getting the evening meal ready she said, "Tell us, Melis, where did you find our friend?"

"Well," Melis said, "you know, our brother in tribulation"— pointing at Harm Hiddesz, who himself was very anxious to get some explanation—"was expected in Leyden, at Folkert's, outside the Gibbet Gate. And we had already looked forward, right Hannes?" he continued, turning to his brother-in-law, "to hear our friend speak during the Christmas days, when I learned in the market place that the bloodhounds of the Inquisition had gotten wind of our meetings. Maybe they had not received correct information and so they thought they could get all of us at once. At any rate, on Thursday night Folkert's house was completely surrounded and soon our faithful friend was taken in chains to the Stone prison. Just when I was talking about this sad happening, the sheriff, followed by his armed men, entered the Fish Market, and there he read that 'Harm Hiddesz, better known as the Peddler,' was suspected to be in hiding in Leyden, and that every citizen and burgher was duty bound, on penalty of complicity, to deliver him up to the court. At the same time a reward of twenty Carolus guilders was promised to anyone who could supply information that would lead to his capture.

"Now I don't know why, but when on my way back from the Dam I stopped in at the ferryhouse for a few minutes, it was as if an inner voice told me that the strange traveler who was sitting there might be Harm and, going straight to the point, I called him by his name and brought him over here."

"And you did well, Melis, by doing what you did," Hannes said.

Harm Hiddesz was deeply touched. Although he was used to being continually in danger, the thought nevertheless shook him that not only he, but also his sick son, would have fallen into the hands of the highhanded Inquisition had not his faithful God who watched over him sent Melis at the right time to meet him.

"Indeed," the woman said, "the Lord watches over His people. In these days of great tyranny, He will establish the words of the prophet Isaiah, chapter 27: 'In that day there shall be a vineyard of red wine; sing ye of it by turns. I the Lord do keep it; I will water it every moment; lest the enemy hurt it, I will keep it night and day.'"

Harm Hiddesz looked up in surprise.

"You marvel at that," Hannes said, "but let me tell you that my wife can read as well as the best clerk or secretary — something that can be said of few men, and still fewer women, of our kind. When in her youth she was one of the maidservants of the lord of Duivenvoorde, she did profit from the lessons the old chaplain of the castle gave her, and because she learned quickly, the old priest who, between you and me, more or less ate the bread of charity there, took a liking to her and taught her how to read and write. My brother Melis and I can't do either, so Mother must do it for us."

"Now you are making too much of my knowledge, Father; nevertheless, if I am grateful for what the old chaplain taught me, then it is especially because it enables me, also for you, to learn from Scripture what is necessary for our salvation.

"And I should tell you also that we, only because the lord of Duivenvoorde is always very considerate of me, have thus far escaped all the troubles which otherwise the priest of Voorschoten might have given us. Although the final jurisdiction resides with the 'lords of The Hague,' nevertheless no 'ordinance of the criminal court' can be given us without his will and approval."

"What learned words you use, Mother dear! This shows you, master Harm, that my wife really studied at the castle!"

"Come, let us sit down and eat," the woman said; "and you, master Harm, will you lead us in prayer? But where is Bouke?"

Just then Bouke entered the room. It was the little fellow whom we already momentarily have met before. In the candlelight his face looked almost frightening because of his misshapen and distorted features. Smallpox had left its deep marks, and wide scars lay here and there across his cheeks. One eye was completely gone and he could hardly open the other on account of the heavy upper lid. His hair was cropped short and made his head seem larger than it was; and his mouth, never closed on account of his deformed lips, showed teeth that looked more like those of an animal than of a human being. His face reflected nothing but ignorance, whereas its heavy bones betrayed gigantic strength.

Harm Hiddesz, who had not said anything yet, looked with some repugnance at the face that was far from winsome.

Hannes's wife noticed it and smiled to herself.

"Bouke," she said, "this, now, is Harm Hiddesz whom we talked about some time ago."

An Unexpected Hiding Place

At the mention of this name, Bouke just stood there, bewildered, bashfully turning his cap around in his hands.

"Master Harm," the woman continued, "Bouke is a true friend in whose heart God has commenced to glorify His grace. In his youth he was my playmate and the scars on his face are badges of honor for which many a knight would envy him. When the home of my parents was struck by lightning, he saved me at the peril of his own life; and afterwards, while helping to save our things, the burning roof fell on him and he was caught underneath it for some time so that he will bear the marks of it for the rest of his life. And if he had to, he would go through a fire for me again, wouldn't you, Bouke?"

Bouke did not know what to answer to these words of praise, so he took his place at the table, and Harm Hiddesz offered a prayer before the meal as had been requested.

While all were helping themselves from the one dish that stood in the center of the table, the woman suddenly stood up, saying, "We almost forgot the child!"

"I don't think he will want anything to eat, good woman," Harm said. "Besides, I have been listening all the while whether he were calling me. The poor lad needs his rest because the past couple of days we have wrestled through have been bad indeed."

So the meal was continued. When all were finished, Harm walked over to his satchel which stood in a corner of the room and loosened its straps. When the satchel was opened he took all kinds of articles out of it — colored linen and woolen cloths, small pieces of jewelry, knives and combs, buttons and ribbons, in short, all kinds of things that were able to tempt many a young farmer or farmer's daughter to buy. The peddler, however, indifferently laid all these things aside. When he reached the bottom, he removed that too, and there appeared, neatly arranged, a small supply of books which no one would have expected to be there underneath all the trinkets.

Among these books there was a copy of *Het Offer des Heeren*, a book which as far as is known saw already in 1599 its eleventh edition.

Then there was the *Liedekens-bouck*, in which you will find manifold songs, both old and new; further, a profitable and comforting booklet on faith and hope, and what true faith is, printed at Antwerp by Adriaen van Berghen (1543). And finally, a few *Testaments* by men and women who for their faith had given their lives on the scaffold or at the stake.

These testaments, or letters of admonition as they were often called, deserve to be discussed in some detail.

Generally speaking, the measure of liberty which prisoners enjoyed in the days of our story was greater than today. At any rate, they were allowed to write, and it was hoped that the writings of the prisoners would contain information that would be helpful to apprehend accomplices or fellow believers. When we remember, moreover, that many prisoners for the sake of their faith had to testify in writing to many of the Inquisition's questions, then it is not surprising that the *Book of Martyrs* so often makes mention of such letters written in prison. History even relates that in very severe cases, when ink was withheld from the prisoners, some, like a certain Joris Wippe, wrote their last letters to their children with "juice of mulberries," and some even with their own blood.

The prisoners, therefore, were greatly concerned that their closest relatives and friends knew how they felt in their last hour, and they often urged their relatives to be present at their "sacrifice"—their execution. Their courageous faith and steadfastness during their last moments would strengthen and possibly confirm the surviving loved ones in their own faith.

These "testaments," often put in rhyme by the seller, and prefaced with a brief description of the history of the martyr and followed by some letters, were printed in booklets of a very small size. And they found—sometimes already even on the day of execution—many buyers. Hence it is not surprising that they were hid "behind the bedstead or under the roof on account of the great terror of the persecution and the great tyranny," and that they were passed on to fellow believers and first copied. Finally in printed form they were distributed on a large scale.

The prisoners knew how greatly their writings were valued. A certain Jan de Grave, for instance, wrote, "Pass this on to each other and commend it to God; read and reread it diligently and understand it wisely. Ah! if you do this it will be

An Unexpected Hiding Place

manifest that all of you seek your salvation and hold my writing in esteem." Or, as Joriaen Simonsz wrote, "This is my last will and testament to you; this I desire of you, that you will diligently read it through, contemplate upon it, and compare it with Scripture in order to direct your paths thereby." And Godefroy van Hamell, killed in 1552 at Doornik, wrote to his sister in his report of his examination and confession: "Not for this reason, however, that you might be edified and instructed by it, as by a great and perfect wisdom, but consider it as a confession by the least of God's servants who did not wish to bury the talent which he had received from the Lord."

These testaments — of which some are still to be found in the Royal Library — these small, dirty, coarsely printed pamphlets should fill even the unbeliever with reverence when he pages through them. If only these pamphlets could speak!

Nor was it surprising that the government kept a sharp eye on the distribution of them and did all it could to prevent this; but it is just as understandable that everyone who had embraced the Reformation eagerly stretched out his or her hands to these fruits that were forbidden by the government.

But however venerable and desirable these writings were, Harm Hiddesz carried still better testaments in his satchel. He had three sets of the Holy Scriptures in four small volumes of the well-known edition of that time with him. He now took one of these volumes and, still under deep impression on account of the unexpected help offered him and especially his sick child, he read from it the seventeenth chapter of the first book of Kings to them.

"What did you just read there, master?" the farmer's wife asked after Harm had finished. "My part of the Holy Scriptures does not contain that."

Then, knowing to be amongst friends, she went to the alcove where Adriaan was sleeping and got from a secret place a little book that was of the same size as those Harm carried in his satchel. Harm took it in his hands and paged through it for a few moments.

"My dear woman," he said, "this is only a part of Holy Scripture, and fortunately I am in the position to offer you the missing parts. The volume you have is one of four that have been published in Antwerp between the years 1525 and 1527. The small size in which the Scriptures are printed is certainly very convenient to hide them, and as you see I always have a supply on hand. I gladly give you the missing volumes."

Mrs. Hannes was in the clouds.

"Look, Father!" she exclaimed, "we considered ourselves rich already, but now we have a mine of inexhaustible riches. Oh dear sir, how can I show you my gratitude?"

"By diligently reading the books," Harm replied seriously. "They do not cost me anything because I regularly receive at certain times of the year new supplies for distribution; and as you see I am not stingy with them."

Once they had started discussing Scripture, Harm had to tell more and more about it. And he did this gladly for he had accepted it as his calling in life to further the extension of God's kingdom as much as lay in his power. Thus talking, they quite naturally arrived at the life's story of Harm himself.

3

What Harm Hiddesz Related

Hannes and Melis, as well as the woman, wished to learn how Harm Hiddesz had been brought on the way which so many had already sprinkled with their blood. At their request he told them the following:

"My father was a cheese merchant, from Frisian descent. He had a small store in the Achterom in the Hague which my mother took care of while my father made the rounds visiting the farmers; he had customers as far away as Antwerp. Although our store was well-known in the city, nevertheless my father often earned more in one day than my mother in a whole week. Hence, I too was trained for this trade and after my father's death I visited the faraway customers, just as he had done before. When I was twenty-three years old, I married a Flemish girl. Since she could hardly be put in charge of our small store, my mother remained in the business, and we moved into a home not far from the Beguine Cloister, on the corner of the Spui.

"I had not been married for three months yet, when I noticed that my wife entertained certain ideas concerning some religious matters that were entirely strange to me. I could not exactly determine that she entertained heretical ideas, but it soon appeared to me that she had different convictions regarding many things from what we had always learned and believed.

"So, soon we had many an argument, in which she always turned out to be the winner by quoting Scriptures that were unknown to me. At first I was seized with fear. Had I unknowingly married a heretical woman? Yet it did not spoil the fine relationship that existed between us. In church, to be sure, we were continually warned against the 'heretical doctrines' that slowly drifted across the borders and entered our country, but at that time the government did not keep such a sharp eye on these things, and the placards were not as severe then as they are now.

"In the course of the first few years of our marriage, however, I had absorbed many heretical teachings. During my frequent visits to Antwerp and Flanders, which often lasted for several weeks, I frequently came in contact with burghers who openly dared to admit that they read the Bible and other books which we were forbidden to read. Whenever I asked my wife, back home, if she had ever heard others read from such books, she seemed hesitant at first, and not inclined to answer my questions frankly. Bit by bit, however, I learned that she had frequented the circles where these books were known, although they were not allowed in her father's house.

"Our eldest little son was about eight years old when our second child, a darling little girl of about five, was stricken with a dread children's disease. Everybody fled and avoided our house except a cousin on my father's side by the name of Anne-Bet, who loved our little daughter dearly. So she assisted my wife and was the only one who stayed with us.

"The help of the physician, however, brought no improvement in the condition of the sick little one. After fearful suffering the dear child succumbed at last." Harm Hiddesz wiped a tear from his eye. Even now, after so many years, the heart of the father ached when he thought of his child. Hannes's wife, too, was greatly touched and filled with deep sympathy.

Harm continued, "With the death of our little daughter a new period set in for us. Our cousin Anne-Bet as well as my wife seemed beyond the reach of comfort. 'Now this is your deserved punishment that has come upon you,' she once said to my wife. 'All the vows I have vowed to Our Lady and my patron saint in behalf of the dear child have been to no avail. And why not? Because you, like most of the strangers that come here, have become totally or partly heretic. Do you think I have not noticed that already a long time ago? Your husband may be blind to it, but not I. What have you done for the dear child? You have taken good care of her; you have hardly been out of the clothes you now have on. All this is fine and good; and I expect that of a good mother. But you have not offered even the smallest candle in the chapel on the bridge!'

"I had expected that my wife would angrily tell our cousin Anne-Bet to keep her mouth closed, but to my amazement she did not do so. Instead she burst out in tears again. 'Ah,' she said, 'if this is indeed my deserved punishment, then it must be on account of my sin and guilt. Quite a long time ago already the way of salvation was pointed out to me and I have renounced the worship of idols and all the idle show of the church when I, out of love for my husband, tried to choke the germ of a beginning new life in my heart. Yes, and now the Lord is against me and strikes me in the dearest possession I have, to show me that I loved flesh and blood more than Him and esteemed them higher than the honor of His Name.'

"Upon hearing these words, I stood as if I were petrified. Anne-Bet threw her arms up in the air in astonishment. 'Didn't I tell you?' she cried. 'Now it comes out! But you are not keeping me any longer in this house. The priest only recently said, Reject every heretic!'

"So Anne-Bet left our house. A few hours later I went to see her. I told her that maybe she had been a little too hasty in her judgment. I called her attention to the sorrows that rent the heart of my wife as mother; and I made her clearly understand that she would ruin not only my wife, but also me and my child if she were going to tell everybody and everywhere that my wife was a heretic. At my urgent plea she finally promised me that she would not tell anybody anything. Alas, I did not know then how evil and horrible the heart of a person is who has not discovered by the light of the Holy Spirit who he or she is, nor has been drawn to Him by the chords of His love.

"From that moment on, my wife, who almost completely secluded herself from the world, expressed and defended her convictions regarding the truth more and more, and she spared no effort to win me too for the cause of the Lord.

"Yet I remained deaf to her entreaties. I observed the holy days of the church, and even went to church once in a while; but for the rest I was, in short, a rather indifferent Roman Catholic and still far removed from true Christianity. Something else had to take place to shake me awake and to make me discover who and what I was.

"A year after the death of my little daughter another son was born — the young lad who is sleeping there in the alcove. My mother had died in the meantime and the store had passed over into the hands of strangers. It was just at the time that I was ready to go on my second annual trip to Brabant and Antwerp. My wife, who at other times was always resigned and quiet when I had to leave her for a few weeks, was uneasy and sad this time, and if I had listened to her, I would have cancelled the trip. Since there was no real reason to do so, however, and the interests of my business and my family demanded my absence, I tenderly said goodbye to my wife and my eldest son, a sturdy, healthy-looking boy who had been named after my father, Hidde. My wife then laid little Adriaan in my arms and I kissed the child who, crowing, stretched his little hands out to me.

"I don't know why, but when I reached the threshold of my house, I turned back to embrace my wife once more. 'Will you remember to bring me what you promised me, when you come back?' she asked again. And I repeated my promise that I would bring her a little Bible from Antwerp.

"My trip was not only pleasant but it was also very profitable. I had made new business contacts and all I had to do after my return home was to see to it that large quantities of cheese, which were ready and waiting for me in the homes of the farmers, were shipped. In Antwerp I did not have much trouble buying the book which my wife wanted so badly. That night, when I arrived at the inn where I usually stayed, I could not resist my curiosity to glance through the book which we laymen are forbidden to read. I paged through it and read a bit here and there until suddenly my attention was drawn to the words, 'Cursed is every one that continueth not in all things which are written in the book of the law to do them.' Those words went through my soul like an arrow, and shook me to the core. Cursed was everyone that did not do the things written in God's law! That was too much for me! I put the book back in my suitcase and went downstairs to the barroom to divert my thoughts; but neither the noisy brawling of the customers nor the wine which I drank in large quantities were able to drown the voice that continually repeated inside of me, 'Cursed, cursed!'"

No one uttered a word to distract Harm Hiddesz while he was telling his story. They all followed him with rapt attention, and the farmer's wife showed her agreement by a constant nodding of her head. Bouke, who was leaning with his arms on the table and holding his deformed head between his big calloused hands, could not keep his one eye from the speaker. From time to time he growled softly, which was his usual way of showing great interest.

"I could not stand it any longer downstairs," Harm Hiddesz continued. "I went back upstairs again, compelled as it were to pick up the book again. Was that why my wife had to have that book, to read every day that she was cursed? But would it not be the right thing to do, then, to observe one's religious duties faithfully and by good works make up for one's shortcomings? Did not Holy Mother Church have a store of good works at her disposal, left her by the saints as a precious heritage? These thoughts calmed me down somewhat. So again I paged through the book. Then my eye fell on the words of Ephesians 2: 'For by grace are ye saved through faith.' The more I read, the less I understood of it. How was that — could good works add nothing to or detract nothing from my salvation? I became more and more confused. The law preached damnation to me, and the gospel closed for me the sources which the church always held open for us. But one thing stayed with me — good works availed nothing, and the word 'Cursed!' continually resounded in my ears. At last I went to bed, but sleep did not come. For the first time I realized why the church forbade laymen to read Scripture! I decided to wait until

I got home, very anxious to hear how my wife, who knew more about the Bible, would solve these contradictory matters.

"The next day I boarded a boat to cross the Scheldt River in order to go back to Holland. Even before it was night, we had to battle against a furious northwesterly wind. As you possibly know, the Scheldt under such conditions is very turbulent and, on account of the shallow places here and there, very dangerous. The strong wind grew into a storm. The large boat was wrenched loose from its anchor and our lanterns were extinguished by the water that beat wildly across the deck. Soon we ran aground and all the while the waves pounded incessantly against the weak sides of the old, dilapidated boat. Tense with fear we looked at the skipper. This fear changed to desperate terror when we saw him and his two helpers bare their heads and kneel, and heard them pray for help to the Virgin Mother and all the saints. Mechanically, I too fell down on my knees. But again the word 'Cursed!' resounded in my ears. It seemed as if every gust of wind screamed 'Cursed, cursed!' One moment later the boat shook again and all of us were thrown against the deck. In my fear I grabbed the railing, but another wave bigger and stronger than the previous one rolled across the deck, dragging the railing and me along with it in its shattering speed.

"I can hardly describe what went on in my mind during those moments. I felt that this was going to be the end. For a second I saw the image of my wife and children before my eyes, but even that impression was pushed aside by the awful sound of 'Cursed!' that pursued me even in the water. I wanted to scream, 'Mercy!' but the roaring water drowned out my voice. I closed my eyes and fainted.

"How long I remained in the water I do not know, but when I came to, I was lying in the middle of a small fisherman's cottage. Two men, one of whom was quite old already, had undressed me and were busy rubbing me.

"'That helps, Father,' the younger of the two said, and he gave me another swallow of a spirituous drink.

"'Thank you!' was all I could utter. I felt so worn out, so exhausted, that I could hardly lift my hands.

"'And now to bed!' the old man said. Then both men lifted me up as if I were a child and carried me to their bedstead.

"But instead of being well again the next day, I had high fevers. To make a long story short, it took more than two weeks before I could get up again. The fishermen, both father and son, had gone through a lot on account of me during that time. I could tell that it made the old man feel good to be able to place me in a chair outside in front of the door in the warm sunshine.

"'The Lord saved you for the second time from death, fellow,' the old man said gravely.

"I looked at him rather confusedly.

"'Just think,' he continued, 'what would have been your fate if you had fallen into other hands than those of brethren, for if this had been found on you' (he got out the little Bible I had bought for my wife) 'then most likely you would have been languishing in prison as a heretic.'

"I was startled. In my agitated condition I had put the little book in the pocket of my jerkin that last night in Antwerp, and it was all that was left of the few possessions I had carried aboard the boat.

"'You need not be alarmed, friend,' continued the old man. 'You notice that I know the value of the book. I have let it dry; like your clothes, it was soaked through and through.'

"'Then you will be able to tell me more about this book,' I said, because I remembered again all the emotions which the reading of Scripture had evoked in me.

"The old man, who had taken me for a follower and professor of the new doctrine, looked up in surprise. I told him my story — about my wife and about the terrifying moments I had experienced before he found me, exhausted, on the shore when in my unconsciousness I was hanging on to the chunk of wood, to which next to God I owed my life.

"The old fisherman, a man who had been on the way to heaven for many years and who already at the dawn of the Reformation had found the Lord, instructed me and taught me to understand the Scripture. No doctor in theology at the University of Louvain could have competed with him. He had never dug his way through the tomes which the church fathers, worthy of our esteem though they may be, had left us but instead, had been taught by the Lord and daily received new light and instructions from the Holy Spirit who leads His people into all truth.

"For him all contradictions dissolved in a childlike faith, and if I had not longed for home, for wife and children, I would have stayed for weeks at the God-fearing fisherman's house.

"I bade a fond farewell to him and his son. A reward they did not want. Besides, I had nothing to offer them at that moment anyway. I promised them, however, to visit them again soon, a promise which I have kept by frequently looking them up.

"After an absence of more than seven weeks, I disembarked at the Spui from the boat which had taken me from Rotterdam to The Hague. With a pounding heart I hastened home.

"When I got near my house, I saw something strange. What was the meaning of that? The shutters were closed; and after frequent rapping on the door, it did not open. I was struck. It seemed that all my blood flowed back to my heart. My knees trembled and my teeth chattered.

"Then a few houses away a door opened. The woman who came out was startled and let out a scream when she saw me standing there. Soon, however, she came to me.

"'Come with me to my house, Harm Hiddesz,' she said.

"I entered and the first thing I saw was my little Adriaan who was quietly sleeping in his cradle.

"'Mrs. Bartels!' I cried, 'where is my wife?' She covered her face with her hands and did not answer."

Then Harm Hiddesz' voice started to tremble so that he could hardly continue. Hot tears rolled between his fingers which he had pressed against his eyes. No one around him attempted to disturb the silent grief of the peddler.

Bouke was still sitting in the same position, without stirring, at the table. He too, seemed deeply touched because a big tear gleamed in the sparse light of the candle in his one, half-closed eye.

Harm Hiddesz soon pulled himself together and continued in a trembling voice, "Forgive me, friends, if I do not go into all the details of the calamity that had befallen me. During my absence my wife had become seriously ill when she had heard the rumor that I had drowned with a skipper on the Scheldt.

She developed a vehement brain fever and two days after the sad news had reached her she died.

"Mrs. Bartels, out of sympathy, had taken my youngest child, cradle and all, into her home. Anne-Bet had seen to it that my wife was buried after she had received the administration of a priest whom my cousin hastily had summoned during the last hours, although my wife was unconscious already. After that the bailiff had locked up the house and taken the key with him.

"Before I went to see the bailiff, however, I ran like a madman to the house of Anne-Bet. But from her neighbors I learned that she had left; nobody knew where she had gone.

"'And what about my child, my Peter?' I cried.

"'She took the little boy with her,' was the reply. Everything turned black before my eyes; it was as if the ground opened up before my feet, and if the neighbors had not grabbed me, I would have slumped to the ground. After I recovered, I went to the bailiff and asked him where Anne-Bet had gone with my child, but he couldn't answer that question.

"Half an hour later I entered my house again and, weeping loudly, fell down before the bedstead in which my dear wife had breathed her last. I was overwhelmed by a feeling that bordered on despair. I pulled my hair out of my head and rolled about the floor.

"When it started getting dark, Bartels, the husband of the woman who had taken in my youngest child, entered the room. He laid his hand on my shoulder and said, 'Come along, friend, come along with me.'

"I followed willingly.

"'Be a man, and be strong,' he said. Then he took little Adriaan, who was still sleeping, from the cradle and laid him in my arms.

"'Remember that your good wife, God have her soul'—he devoutly made the sign of the cross—'has left you this.'

"I kissed the little one and — all the while sighing and with tears in my eyes — put him back in his cradle.

"The next day I went with my neighbor Bartels to see my wife's grave in St. Jacob's Church. The usual prayer for the soul's rest of the dead refused to come from my lips. I wa still wearing the clothes in which I had arrived, and convulsively I pressed the little book my wife had wanted so badly.

"'By grace are ye saved!' I sighed. Now, for the first time, I began to understand to some extent the soul struggle which she who now lay underneath the cold slab of stone near the main altar had known.

"Within a few days I had sufficiently regulated my business affairs to be able to go on a trip again. The thought of my elder son left me no peace.

"I considered it praiseworthy that Anne-Bet, thinking that I had drowned, had taken care of my eldest boy, but that she had left without telling anybody where she was going perturbed me. So I made preparations to leave while Mrs. Bartels would continue to take care of my younger child.

"I assumed that Anne-Bet could have gone nowhere else but to her sister who lived in 's-Hertogenbosch. I traveled as fast as I could, and soon found her sister, but not a trace of Anne-Bet or my child. I returned to The Hague, at my wit's end. I questioned everybody, left and right, but I did not get one step closer to my goal. I searched and searched for months, but neither Anne-Bet nor my child could be found."

"But that is terrible!" exclaimed Mrs. Hannes. "And did it take long before you finally found your child?"

"Alas!" Harm Hiddesz sighed, "all my attempts have been in vain. I have never seen my son again! By grace," he continued, "I have willingly suffered hunger and thirst, misery and poverty, scorn and pain, in the service of my God, and nevertheless I know that every moment of rest and peace of soul is still an undeserved gift of grace from His hand; but one thing I have desired of Him, and in answer to my prayer I have received the assurance in my soul that I, even if it is to be only once, shall be granted to see my firstborn before I die."

"May the Lord give you the fulfillment of your prayer, brother," Melis said; "for even though I have no children myself, I can to some extent imagine what it must be like to lose a child in such a manner. But what did you do with your younger son?"

"You can understand," continued Harm Hiddesz, "that from then on my life had another goal and took a different direction.

I had no peace. Although I was by no means wealthy, I nevertheless could sell my business quite advantageously. For the time being I left my little Adriaan with the kind, sympathetic neighbor lady who had taken the little fellow into her home. I gave her a small compensation. I took my money for safekeeping to the old fisherman who had saved my life, which, especially in these troubled times, is necessary. There it is as safe as if it were locked behind iron doors. With him, too, I often found a safe hiding place when my pursuers were after me and the safety of my life demanded that I disappear for a time. So I wandered now here, then there, always hoping to discover some trace of my child. Meanwhile, God's grace which in principle had been planted in my heart, continued to grow as the oppression increased; and it was not until later that I learned to understand that through a way of suffering and bitter grief I was brought closer to Him who had chosen me, as I may believe, to be a vessel unto His glory and to disseminate His pure truth."

The little company would have visited together much longer if the woman had not urged them to go to bed now since Harm Hiddesz would stay a few days anyway, if nothing came in between. After having knelt and prayed together, they all retired, Harm finding a welcome place of rest beside his little son.

After breakfast the next morning, while the farmer and his brother with the help of Bouke took care of the cattle, the woman said to Harm Hiddesz, "It is too bad that we did not know sooner that you would spend a few days with us. The friends could very well have come here and it would not have aroused the least suspicion. We live here quite out of the way and, the ice being strong, several people will be visiting each other on skates. What do you think? Would you be willing to speak a word of edification to our friends, even though there are not very many here?"

"Certainly," Harm Hiddesz replied, "and even though they be few, remember that it is written: 'Where two or three are gathered together in My Name, there am I in the midst of them.' But how will you inform them about it?"

"Just leave that to me!" the woman said, and she hurried at once to the cow-stable where her husband and brother were working.

"Listen, Melis!" she called out, "get on your skates! Harm Hiddesz our guest is going to speak to the friends; so start going as quickly as you can and tell it at 'The Blue House' and at 'The Comb!' Also stop at Geerte's and tell it at Krelis van Dieren's. And if you don't take too long, you can also stop at the miller's in the back polder!"

"When and at what time are the people to come?"

"Well, tonight!"

"Listen here, Mother," Hannes protested, "that won't work. On Christmas Day everybody is on the road, and when people see this one and that one stop at our place, we may get visitors in the house whom we cannot very well refuse and who may betray us. 'Be ye therefore wise as serpents, and harmless as doves,' Scripture says, so let us not loosen still further the evil tongues that are wagging so much already. I would therefore be in favor of getting together on the day after Christmas, and then not too late; what do you think of six o'clock in the early evening? Then it will be quite dark already."

After some protest from the woman it was decided to postpone the meeting until the following day.

When Hannes's wife entered the room again to tell Harm Hiddesz about the agreement, she found him sitting at the bedside of his son. The lad had been restless all during the night and had stayed in bed at the request of his father.

Harm Hiddesz looked at his child with eyes that reflected great concern. The fever had seized him again and now much more severely than the night before.

"What can be the matter with the little fellow?" asked the sympathetic woman.

"I think that he has caught a severe cold and that he could not stand the walking and traveling of these last days."

"Why didn't you leave the little one behind with some good friends who could take care of him? It seems to me that he is too young to accompany you all the time. And I don't think he is any too strong, the poor lad!"

"I don't intend to take him with me wherever I go," Harm Hiddesz replied. "When Adriaan was about six years old, I had to take him away from the people in The Hague. They had been very good to the child, but I could not allow him to be brought up in the papist teachings. For the time being I took him to my old friend the fisherman. There he had it very good. You understand that I saw to it that he lacked nothing; but he could not always remain there either. During my recent visit to Emden I made arrangements with a certain family, to whom I can entrust my child wholeheartedly, that I would take Adriaan there in the interest of his upbringing and his future. He wept when he had to say goodbye to the old fisherman, which proves how good he had had it there.

"When I arrived in Rotterdam, I learned that it was not safe to stay there. I had to leave the city in a hurry in order not to fall into the hands of the Inquisition which — how I don't know — had gotten wind of my presence. I got a ride on a farmer's cart to The Hague, but from there I had to walk to Leyden where I was expected at Folkert's. I had thought to be able to stay in Leyden until the water was open again, and would have traveled with my child through Friesland to Emden. You yourselves know that the Lord's ways are not according to our human way of reckoning."

Fortunately, Adriaan did not lack tender care. The farmer's wife, who felt very sorry for the lad, treated him as though he were her own child, the more so since her own marriage in spite of her great desire was not blessed with children.

Although this Christmas Day was very pleasant for the small group of friends, we shall not describe it in detail but continue our story with recounting the following day, which Roman Catholics still call St. Stephen's Day.

4

A Remarkable Sermon

At the time Hannes had indicated, the large room which served as the living room was filled with farmers and farmers' wives, artisans, and some servants from the distant Duivenvoorde Castle. Although it had not taken Melis very long to reach the friends of the new doctrine even though some lived quite far away, the news that Harm Hiddesz was going to speak at Hannes's house was nevertheless passed very secretly from one to another in a whisper. And as Hannes's wife had remarked, the ice was good and in those days nearly everybody could and did skate.

Mrs. Hannes had not had so much company in many years. She tried to give everybody a decent seat; benches were carried in for the women and empty barrels for the men to sit on. Soon even the front room, which contained the cooling trough, was filled with visitors.

It must be emphasized that it was not without good reason that the prudent farmer Hannes had chosen St. Stephen's Day for this meeting. For this day was generally considered a holiday on which people visited each other and on which good food and drink were served. In case the attention of a passing farmer was drawn by the many visitors who went to Hannes's house, or by the singing coming from his house, his suspicion would soon have vanished by remembering the customary gaiety on St. Stephen's evening.

Listen, however, to the nature of the joyfulness of the assembled guests! They were singing a *liedeke* that testified of their joy and trust of faith:

> *Rejoice, believers, one and all;*
> *Though you in number may be small,*
> *No foe can harm or molest you.*
> *If God defend us, we can't fall;*
> *Who, then, is able to assail you?*
>
> *No fortress is as strong as He;*
> *Lord, wilt Thou my Protector be*
> *From evil foes who rage and seethe?*
> *Deliver, my security,*
> *Me from the roaring lions' teeth.*
>
> *Lord, strong in battle, Thou art King,*
> *And victory to us wilt bring;*
> *Oh God, my heart yearns to be near Thee.*
> *Look on Thy servant's suffering;*
> *Call him into Thy kingdom with Thee.*[1]

After the singing Harm Hiddesz appeared from the little alcove, where he had spent some moments at the bedside of his sick son Adriaan, and entered the room. He greeted the visitors, shook hands with a few farmers whom he had met before during his many wanderings, and then took his place behind the big, heavy table on which Hannes's wife had placed a few more candles than usual because of this special occasion.

After a simple yet very stirring prayer, during which Harm as well as all the other men were standing, Harm began his message.

For centuries, he told them, it had been the custom of the Christian church to relate the story of the martyr's death of Stephen on the day after Christmas. Although he and his friends were considered to be professors of a new doctrine, he did not know of a better way to refute this wrong idea than by refusing to depart from this old custom. For what they wanted was not a new religion, but reformation of a church that was steeped in ignorance and superstition.

Then Harm Hiddesz opened his Bible — the one he once

---
[1] Re-rhymed translation of an entry in *Veelderhande Liedekens* of 1569.

had bought in Antwerp for his wife and which had never left him since. He first read part of Luke 2 and after that Acts 6:8ff.

After Harm Hiddesz had called the friends' attention to the fact that on Christmas Day they had seen and heard the great mercy of God in the birth of His Son and the great comfort and joy the believers of all ages might derive from it, he continued thus:

"But since it is man's nature that he can hardly be satisfied with this joy but often under the pretense of a godly joy adds to it a worldly or vain joy, therefore the old fathers justly decreed that this day was to be observed after the day of the commemoration of the birth of Christ, and for this reason, that man would not spend it in intemperateness or worthless jollity. For we see — and may God change it — that just like the godly forefathers decreed that the blessed birth of Christ must be commemorated each year so that man would keep it forever in his memory, so Satan on the other hand has worked in the opposite direction by instituting evenings of fun on November 18 and January 20, on which people come together to eat and drink excessively and to act foolishly so that the great mercy of this blessed birth would be forgotten as soon as possible. And these evenings are called 'good evenings'; indeed, friends, they could justly be called 'fools' nights', for it is foolishness to barter this heavenly joy for temporal joy.

"Thus Satan has corrupted everything, for as soon as we commemorate the blessed resurrection of Christ for our justification — from which we should learn how much He has done for us, and that this remembrance or commemoration of His bitter death must always be in our hearts and minds — immediately the day after Easter Satan offers a fair outside the city where people go prancing, some to show off their beautiful clothes; others to get drunk; still others to decorate and deck themselves out; and all this in such a way that souls might be deceived. All these things Satan does to turn men's attention away from godly meditations, for Satan knows that as long as men's hearts are full of thoughts about the divine blessings of His suffering, he has no room nor place in their hearts. But in order to prevent this evil bird from immediately picking up the seed from the soil of the heart; and that the believing, newborn children may let it sink in deeply so that it takes root and bears fruit, we shall learn from this text that for which those who accept and are united with Christ — also this newborn child — usually await. For Christ is everywhere an offense to the Jews and foolishness unto the Greeks. And in order that those who welcome Christ the newborn King, on Christmas Day, count the cost thereof and realize what His believers await — so that they would not think later on that they had been deceived — we shall, by the grace of God, consider a true example in this holy and blessed man Stephen."

We cannot follow Harm Hiddesz's whole sermon, but our readers are sufficiently acquainted with the manner of preaching of our first evangelical witnesses in those days; hence it is sufficient that we mention that Harm Hiddesz's speech that night sparkled with the fire of the Spirit and the power of his faith.

It was no wonder, therefore, that the audience hung, as it were, on his lips. It was so seldom that they heard words such as these, and since they hungered after the Bread of Life, they defied all the punishments threatened by the placards of the tyrannical government, in order to catch a few crumbs of that Bread.

The speaker continued for a long time until he concluded with the following words, "Therefore, oh all ye elect children and beloved of the Lord, ye who hope for His comfort and for deliverance, who indeed have felt concern and uneasiness concerning your souls, praise and thank the merciful Father who sends you the Savior, yes, the Peacemaker. So let us embrace Him on this joyful day; let us commemorate His birth and pray that He may be born in our hearts and celebrate His feast because that will result in eternal joy; for without His birth in us, Christmas will avail us very little even if we observed it every day. But if we have received this grace, He will come and dwell in us together with the Father and the Holy Spirit. May the merciful Father grant us this grace through Jesus Christ, this newborn Child who, together with the Father and the Holy Spirit, lives and triumphs eternally. Amen."

With a short prayer he then concluded the meeting.

When everybody made ready to leave, an old farmer walked up to the preacher and, placing a gold coin into Harm's hand, he said, "For the brethren in tribulation; golden words may not be paid for with copper."

5

The Heretic Hunt

Little did the assembled brethren suspect that their gathering had aroused the curiosity of someone who was anything but a friend of theirs.

Aart, the farmer who had so mercilessly refused Harm Hiddesz a few moments by the hearth before he had reached the ferryhouse with his sick son, earlier in the evening while skating towards the home of one of his friends, had met several people who had only casually answered his "good ev'ning." And, turning his head, he had noticed that they all went in the direction of Hannes's house.

This greatly aroused his curiosity.

"What's going on at Hannes's?" he thought. "He seldom gets that much company!"

When after a couple of hours he returned home, it seemed that the wind carried the sounds of singing over to him.

"Didn't that come from Hannes's place?"

He cocked his ears. Again he was overcome by curiosity and could not resist the temptation to turn into the frozen watercourse that led to Hannes's house.

The farm dog started to bark, but inside nobody paid attention to it because they were all listening with rapt attention to the speaker and, besides, many a farmer from the neighborhood had passed by the house on his skates.

Aart sneaked carefully underneath one of the windows. What he saw through the cracks of the blinds amazed him greatly. He could hear someone speak, but could not make out what was said. Nor could he see the speaker; but he did see several people he knew and they were all quietly sitting in a row, seemingly listening with rapt attention to the speaker.

Aart did not understand it.

"What may be the meaning of this?" he muttered, and would have liked to peer much longer. But then he saw a woman stand up and, thinking that she would be coming outside to quiet the dog which was tied to his chain and kept on barking, he sped away on his skates and soon reached the Vliet.

He had to pass the ferryhouse. Maybe there he could learn more about this; at any rate he could talk about this strange thing with the ferryman. It must be remembered that especially in the country every happening, no matter how insignificant in itself, was apt to bring some stirring in the everyday life of a farmer or villager.

The ferryman could of course give no explanation; they were making all kinds of guesses when the silence outside was disturbed by the thud of horses' hoofs.

Both the ferryman and Aart ran outside. Horsemen that late in the evening along the Vliet was such an unusual thing that the meeting at Hannes's house was nothing compared to it.

The horsemen, three in number, drew in the reins when they came to the ferryhouse.

"Hey there, lout!" cried the first one, "is this an inn?"

"Right you are, noble lords!" the ferryman answered, bowing humbly. With his sharp innkeeper's eye he had quickly noticed that these men were no ordinary guests.

"Wouldn't the gentlemen rather get off for a few minutes? I have a very good stable to keep the horses warm."

"What do you think, Antonio?" the first rider asked the one beside him.

"Must you ask yet? All day long we haven't done anything else but run back and forth, and in this kind of weather. Truly, if I had known that it could be that cold in this country of frogs, which you always call that glorious Holland, I would have stayed in the south!" And without adding another word, the man whose name was Antonio, as we overheard, jumped out of the saddle.

The third horseman, seeing this, was soon standing on the ground too, and grabbed the reins of Antonio's horse.

"Take them inside, Sjoerd!" cried one of the men. Aart, who from curiosity was now extremely obliging, led the way, and soon the steaming horses were put up in the stable behind the ferryhouse, the place where the horses that pulled the towing-barges were often fed in summer.

Then he and Sjoerd entered the barroom where the two other horsemen were already seated, each with a large mug of beer in front of him.

Now that they had doffed their long riding mantles, one could see by their whole outfit and by the long rapier they carried on their sides that they were soldiers; and it was evident from their commanding tone of voice when speaking to Sjoerd that the latter was their servant and hence that they must occupy a certain rank in the army of the governess of the country.

"Come here a minute, innkeeper!" called the first one who appeared to be the most important of the three.

The ferryman walked up to him.

"I have a question to ask, but tell me no lies and give me no excuses, do you hear, or"— and he slapped his sword so that Aart's heart jumped with fright—"you will know with whom you are dealing!"

The ferryman, however, did not bat an eye.

"Just ask, noble lord, and I will tell you the truth," he said quietly.

The officer continued, "Did a man recently pass by with a peddler's pack or something? Don't lie!"

"Often traveling peddlers of that kind pass by here," the ferryman replied, "although at this time of the year not as frequently as in summer."

"I am not asking who passes by here in summer!" was the barking reply, "but whom have you seen here in the last couple of days?"

The ferryman acted as if he was consulting his memory.

"Wait a minute!" he said, "the day before yesterday a man like that stopped in here. He had a young boy of about twelve with him!"

The one horseman looked at his friend Antonio. "That can't be the one," he said, shaking his head.

Antonio shrugged his shoulders. It did not seem to interest him in the least. All he answered was, "I wish this brown detestable stuff was Malvoisy wine!" and he pushed the beer mug disdainfully away from him.

The ferryman, who wanted to put the guests who had arrived so late in the evening in a good mood, asked, "Maybe the chief can give a more detailed description of the person whom he seeks?"

The officer looked sharply at the ferryman for a moment, then said, "You are a good Catholic, aren't you?"

"Nobody ever doubted it," the ferryman proudly answered.

"Well, then," the chief continued, "we are looking for a heretic of the most dangerous kind. According to the information we received, he must have tried to reach Leyden along this way, because he was supposed to hold one of those heretical meetings at which those dogs do nothing but tread on the holy host, and who knows what other abominable things they do there. He did not arrive in Leyden, because they watched closely for him there. And he did not return to The Hague. So he must be somewhere in this neighborhood."

Aart had summoned up enough courage to walk a little closer towards the men. What he heard from the lips of that harsh officer clarified something in his mind. But he still did not have the courage to say a word.

"Just think," the chief continued, "that you can earn a fine rimmed golden ducat and a place in heaven if you can lead us on this accursed heretic's trail."

As good a Roman Catholic as the ferryman might be, the ducat appealed far more to him than a place in heaven. But no matter how he thought and thought, he could offer no further information.

The promised ducat had also a mighty influence on Aart who was commonly called "niggardly Aart." By picturing the golden coin in his mind, he succeeded in conquering his shyness.

"Maybe *I can* show the gentlemen the way," he said timidly.

"Speak up, fellow!" the chief interrupted him. So Aart told what he had seen.

"By St. Martin!" the officer exclaimed, jumping up from the bench on which he was seated. "He must be there! Quick, Antonio, hurry up! Those heretics are as slippery as eels when you try to catch them!"

Antonio seemed to have awakened too during the story Aart had told them.

"We had better leave the horses here," he said, fastening his sword a little higher.

"Of course, we can't very well cross the ice with the animals."

"And you show us the way. When we have that heretic, so help me, my patron saint, you will get the ducat."

Aart walked ahead of the three soldiers. A little distance from Hannes's home he stopped.

"There it is, noble lord!"

"Very well. You go back to the ferryhouse and wait for us there."

The officer and Antonio, followed by Sjoerd, approached the house of Hannes. A few steps away from the house they were stopped, however, by the farm's big watchdog which had been unchained by Bouke just a few minutes earlier.

Barking furiously, the dog leaped at the men. It was impossible for them to proceed, for no matter how they tried to keep the animal away from them, it was in vain.

"Miserable country!" railed Antonio while he again tried to hit the dog which was after his legs, with his rapier. "Imagine, three well-tried soldiers of the king being stopped by such a monster!" And again he struck at it with his sword.

The leader, however, put his hand to his mouth and cried as loudly as he could, "Hey there! Open that door!"

The people inside, however, seemed not at all in a hurry to comply with the officer's request.

"The folks must be sleeping!" Sjoerd ventured to remark.

Again the chief produced his powerful noise which reechoed far and wide across the fields.

But the people inside were not sleeping.

Mrs. Hannes was just clearing away the dishes that had been used for supper when Bouke, who had made his usual rounds, entered, all upset.

"Mrs. Hannes," he said, excitedly, "some men are coming this way along the mill-path, and I can see that they are armed!"

Mrs. Hannes called her husband and Melis, and all three went to the door. There was no doubt about it, these men were coming in the direction of their house, and in the clear moonlight they saw the glittering of their swords.

"Is the dog loose?" Hannes asked.

"Yes," Bouke replied.

"Then let us get inside immediately. We must decide what to do because this visit does not concern us, but our guest!"

They deliberated shortly. Resistance was out of the question; that would only result in bloodshed and later in the gravest difficulties, they all agreed.

Harm Hiddesz was willing to surrender himself into the hands of these men if they were after him.

"I don't want you to get into trouble for my sake," he said. "My heavenly Father, who is a Judge of the widows and a Father of the fatherless, will have mercy upon my child."

Outside the dog barked even more furiously.

The farmer's wife quickly made up her mind. "Quick, Bouke," she whispered, "take Master Harm to your bed in the cowstable;

and you," she continued to the men, "let me handle this. Go to your beds, and wait until I call you."

Neither Hannes nor Melis understood a thing of what the woman had in mind, but knowing her sharp mind, they complied with her commands at once.

Outside the captain cried for the third time. Mrs. Hannes hurried to the door and opened it.

"Call that accursed animal away from here!" a harsh voice cried.

"Hello! Here, Bello!" the woman called, and the dog, obeying the voice he knew so well, came to her, barking all the while; whereupon she immediately chained him near the house.

"Good evening, gentlemen!" the woman said, as kindly as possible, to the men approaching her.

"What's the meaning of letting us wait so long?" the captain asked gruffly.

"The watchdog often starts to bark at night, even when no visitors are expected, and I was just busy taking care of my sick boy. But come in, gentlemen, and please tell me what it is you want."

The three soldiers, not expecting such a calm reception, followed the woman into the living room, while she went to the hallway and called at the top of her lungs, "Hannes, come downstairs; we have visitors!"

"I believe that miserable dog has bitten me through my boot cap," the captain now said, dropping down on a large wooden bench. "Yes, indeed," he continued, folding back the leather top of his wide riding boot; "I am bleeding like an ox!"

"Oh," the woman said, "but the animal can't really be blamed." She hurried to get water and linen which the captain used in such a way that it was clear that this was not the first wound he had ever bandaged.

Meanwhile Antonio and Sjoerd glanced around the room, while Hannes and Melis, not knowing what else to do, stayed at the threshold.

"Is that your husband?" the captain asked.

"Yes, my lord," the woman replied, meanwhile helping him with the bandages. "That one over there is my husband; the other is my brother."

"You did have quite a few visitors tonight, didn't you?" the captain went on.

"On St. Stephen's night we usually have quite a bit of company," the farmer's wife answered evasively.

"But a whole house full of people is not usual," the captain said, looking sharply at her.

"Tut, tut, sir, it was not a house full!"

"Is that man still here whom you took in yesterday?" the captain now asked, intending to confuse her by this sudden direct question.

"Does my lord mean that poor peddler who arrived here dead tired?" the woman asked in an innocent tone of voice.

"Yes; where is he?"

"He is sleeping in the cowstable with the farmhand. We country people have a lot of trouble with those wandering fellows, but we may not refuse a deed of mercy, especially not on Christmas Day. The man looked quite honest."

"That's what you think," the captain interrupted her. Her frank admission made him think that these farmers did not know what a dangerous person they had in their house. "That's what you think," he repeated. "That man is one of the most dangerous heretics that trouble our country. Take me immediately to him!"

Sjoerd unsheathed his short dagger and, following the farmer's wife, the three men went to the stable.

"My wife has lost her mind, or else I don't understand anything of it," Hannes whispered to his brother-in-law.

Melis shrugged his shoulders. The woman's behavior seemed incomprehensible to him too.

At a gesture of the farmer's wife, Bouke remained quietly in his bed which stood in a corner of the stable, while a little farther away Harm Hiddesz lay in a kneeling position in front of a similar bedstead.

"Look at that hypocritical heretic!" shouted the captain and, grabbing Harm Hiddesz by his jerkin, he said, "In the name of the king, you are my prisoner."

Harm Hiddesz got to his feet. He looked at the farmer's wife for a second, but did not say a word. If she was handing him over to save his child, then he would be forever grateful to her, he thought.

Back in the living room Antonio and Sjoerd frisked Harm, but they did not find anything suspicious. The little Bible which always accompanied him was hidden underneath the blankets of Adriaan's bed.

"Where is his satchel?" the captain demanded.

Mrs. Hannes got it. "We always keep those things for these people," she said, "when we give them shelter for the night, because it would not be the first time that in payment for our hospitality we were robbed by them!"

But the satchel, too, contained nothing that could arouse suspicion, and that was no wonder. Even if Harm Hiddesz had had three times as many books with him as he had, they would have been gone by now. The guests would have taken all of them the night before in exchange for liberal payment.

"May I ask what right you have to arrest and examine me?" Harm Hiddesz asked.

"Here's my warrant!" the captain answered, and he produced a parchment which was signed by Del Castro, Provincial Inquisitor of Utrecht. "We followed your trail already from Schoonhoven on, which we lost near Dordrecht, but we found it again in Rotterdam. No matter how smart you are, we know how to get you anyway!"

While the captain was talking, Mrs. Hannes made a show of her utter amazement by all kinds of exclamations and gesticulations.

"And what if you are mistaken in the person?" master Harm asked.

"I never make a mistake!" was the gruff answer; "and even if this would be the case, we can always find out later. Sjoerd, bind this fellow; and then we must be on our way at once!"

A painful expression appeared on the face of the captive, but not because of the narrow leather strap with which Sjoerd tied his wrists together on his back. Rather, the thought that he would never see Adriaan again, that he would have to depart without being able to say goodbye to his child, pierced his soul like a sword. Yet he must suppress his feelings. One word, and he would jeopardize not only the safety but also the life of his child as well. The Inquisition made no distinction in ages!

Mrs. Hannes seemed to feel what went on in Harm Hiddesz's soul, for almost imperceptibly she nodded encouragingly to him.

"But the gentlemen surely are not going to leave like that?" she asked enticingly, looking at the captain. "Come on, Hannes," she continued, turning to her husband, "don't just stand there gaping like that; get the crock out. The gentlemen surely like something to drink that will warm them up in this cold weather."

The captain was an excellent servant and soldier, but the word "crock" never failed to cast a spell over him, especially when he could anticipate that it was filled with something spirituous. Sjoerd too was already pleasantly rubbing his hand across his lips.

Antonio disdainfully pulled his nose up.

"What about him over there?" the captain said, pointing at Harm Hiddesz.

The farmer's wife opened a door that gave entrance to the "best" room. "Lock him up in there for the time being," she said. "The presence of a heretic would spoil the taste of a good drink."

The captain glanced around the room which the woman had opened. It was the "fine" room which was seldom shown to guests. A big, old oak wood linen chest stood against the wall across from the mantelpiece. The only window was protected from burglars by means of iron bars. The hearth opening was covered by a crudely painted wooden board. The open door was the only entrance.

Without further deliberation the handcuffed prisoner was pushed into the dark room.

"If they had come a couple of hours earlier, this would not have gone off so well," Hannes mumbled.

Meanwhile, his wife poured drinks for her guests, and the captain, completely put at ease by the behavior of the woman, and feeling well, enjoyed the intoxicating drink.

She was by no means frugal with it and while talking with the captain about heretics and about Harm Hiddesz, she kept on filling the pewter mugs of the soldiers.

"It does not seem to taste good to my lord," she said to Antonio.

"No, woman, in my country we don't drink this stuff. There we prefer a glass of good wine!"

"Why, dear sir, if I had only known that! I have a large jar of wine in the cellar; you remember, Hannes, the one we got from the lord of the manor, when you were so sick! I am going to fetch it at once!" and, carrying out her intention immediately, she skipped out of the room. But before she descended into the cellar, she went into the cowstable and seeing Bouke who was sitting there, waiting on the edge of his simple bed, she hastily whispered something to him.

The little fellow grimaced. His deformed face became even more distorted on account of the smile that crossed it.

A few moments later Mrs. Hannes was back again and placed the crock of wine on the table.

As it was getting late and the captain kept talking about leaving, she showed signs of restlessness. Hannes, who knew his wife for so many years, noticed that she was not at ease. She was extremely talkative, which to Hannes was an unmistakable sign that she tried to camouflage her uneasiness.

At last the captain, slightly swaying, arose. The other men followed his example.

"And now, good people," he said, "I shall not fail to praise your hospitality to more influential authorities than we are."

"Sjoerd, get the heretic!"

The soldier opened the door through which Harm had entered the room.

There was nobody there!

6

The Clerk of the Inquisitor

The sharp easterly wind which had prevailed for several days had made place for a westerly one. It had stopped freezing and innumerable large snowflakes fluttered down from a heavy gray sky.

With a sad look on his face a young man, dressed in the robes of a priest, was standing in front of one of the many windows of St. Clara Monastery in Leyden.

For a long time he had been standing there, staring out through the small panes of the arched windows, until at last the continual falling of the snowflakes began to bore him.

Dejectedly he took his place at the table which was covered with a green cloth and on which lay a number of parchments with or without large seals beside some pens and a freshly polished pewter inkwell.

"It is strange," he softly said to himself, "but since I have been back in Holland, it is as if I have become another person. Nor do I like the work here. All I ever have to do is writing, writing!" and with a sigh he picked up a goose quill. "It is a wrangling without end with these city councils and magistrates," he continued a little louder. "If they only would let us handle these things, we could much more easily carry out the orders of our illustrious lord and prince which are so clearly laid down in the edicts. But everything we do is thwarted by the obstinacy and pride of these self-willed burghers, as if privileges and local customs are worthy of consideration when the interests of our holy mother and the Church are at stake!"

"That's what I call manly talk, Cornelio!" a voice interrupted him.

Startled, the young priest turned around. He saw a tall, thin, gray-haired priest enter the room by pushing aside the heavy velvet curtain that hung in front of one of the open doorways.

"Forgive me, your reverence, but when one is alone one easily starts to think out loud."

"Here you can do that safely, Cornelio," the old priest replied, "but remember that, generally speaking, it is not a commendable habit."

The cheeks of the blond young man turned scarlet.

"Come, come," the priest said, "I did not mean to scold you, especially not since what you said is an exact interpretation of my own feelings. We cannot make any headway with all these different governing bodies. As soon as we move outside the borders of our own office we meet resistance everywhere. It is seldom that we get cooperation. Every town and every manor has its own particular privileges and woe to us if we touch them. I believe that the people here in Holland would rather see the destruction of our holy religion and the church than to sacrifice and part with one of these so-called liberties.

"I have also noticed that the magistrates here have very little respect for the extensive letters of authorization which I showed them. It would not surprise me one bit if there were quite a number among them who are polluted with this heresy and who are just biding their time for an opportunity to show their true colors. But for the time being you need not be concerned about these problems. Let us rather finish our business so that we will be done by noon."

The gray-headed priest, who had been walking up and down the room when he spoke these words, took a place at the table across from the younger priest whose name, as we overheard, was Cornelio.

As mentioned before, he was a tall, thin man. As canon of St. John's Church in Utrecht, he had on the sixth of May, 1555, taken the place of Lethmate as Provincial Inquisitor. Nicholas Del Castro — this was his name — was in many respects different from his predecessors, especially in his attitude towards the different laws in the places where he was called to carry out his office. In contrast with his predecessors, he always tried to respect the various divergent privileges of the cities and to seek a peaceable solution and agreement between these privileges and the edicts and his authority; and perhaps he owed it to his careful procedure and relative moderation that Granvelle, in his desperate effort to squelch the ever-increasing storm of unrest, rewarded him for his services in 1562 at Malines by appointing him first bishop of Middelburg.

Cornelio was now diligently writing. Although he had only recently been appointed as Del Castro's clerk, the latter had already taken a fatherly interest in him. Born in Holland, Cornelio had become an orphan when quite young. A sympathetic relative had taken him into her care and after the first grief on account of the loss of his parents had subsided somewhat, he had been placed in a monastery, not only to provide him with an excellent education for that time, but also to train him for the priesthood.

At first his teachers had had quite a bit of trouble with him. To be sure, his diligence was great and his conduct exemplary, but the lad had acquired so many strange ideas that were contrary to the teaching of the Roman Catholic Church that it took quite a lot of effort on their part to mold him slowly into a faithful and obedient servant of the church. With much patience and gentleness, however, their objective had been reached. Cornelio, after having studied for three years at the University of Louvain, had been accepted into the priesthood as all signs of heresy had been erased. And whenever they seemed to crop up again, his superiors were ever ready and willing to guide him away from what they considered an erroneous and dangerous road.

Was it possible that they were not completely sure about him on account of possible future deviations from pure Roman Catholic doctrine — or was it purely incidental that Cornelio had been assigned to Del Castro, the man who, although he had a pleasing and easygoing character, was a great defender of the Roman Catholic Church, one whose greatest ambition was the extermination of the Reformation?

Whatever the case, Cornelio put unlimited confidence in Del Castro and followed obediently and unconditionally his advice. He frequently discussed, as is evident from the following conversation, a matter that seemed to be of the greatest importance to him.

"Will we be staying here long, Reverend Father?" Cornelio asked after the last papers had been signed and he was attaching large wax seals to them with narrow strips of parchment.

"That all depends on whether we shall be hearing soon from the Fleming. I don't understand why he does not show up. It seems to me he could have been here a long time ago."

"And when we leave here, we are going to The Hague, aren't we?" Cornelio asked. "I am really anxious to see the place where I was born!"

"I honestly don't know whether I shall be doing the right thing if I take you along there. Maybe memories will come back to you that will disturb your soul's peace."

A look of disappointment spread over Cornelio's face. Nevertheless, he did not dare say anything. If he had been taught one thing, it was obedience, and he was afraid that if he continued he would be diminishing the chance of seeing his wish fulfilled. So he continued his work while Del Castro, deep in thought, paced the floor.

There was a soft knocking at the door at the other side of the room across from the doorway through which Del Castro had entered. Upon Del Castro's permission to enter, a monk appeared, who announced the arrival of the Fleming who requested to see the Reverend Provincial Inquisitor.

"Bring him in at once, brother!" Del Castro said, and a few minutes later the Fleming entered, whom we recognize immediately as the captain who on St. Stephen's night had captured Harm Hiddesz in the home of Hannes.

The Fleming, who was called by that name because he had been born in Antwerp, bowed deeply, holding his narrow-brimmed hat, which was adorned by a couple of rooster feathers, respectfully in his hand.

"Come closer, captain," Del Castro said, with his right hand making the sign of the cross by way of returning the greeting. "You have been long in coming, so I hope you have good news to tell."

"Alas! your reverence," the captain sighed, "I have had bad luck."

Del Castro's face took on a dark expression.

"Explain yourself!" was the short, commanding answer.

The captain started a long story about his traveling back and forth to get on the trail of the heretic who one day played the role of a peddler and the next that of a preacher. When, however, he described his experiences at Hannes's house, and shamefacedly had to admit that at the last moment the heretic had, as it were, slipped through his fingers, Del Castro's anger knew no bounds. He stamped his feet so furiously that even Cornelio was startled.

"That heretic must be in league with Beelzebub," the captain ventured to remark, "because the room had no exit other than to the room in which we were sitting. I never kept my eyes from it while bandaging a wound inflicted by the farmer's mean dog."

The last remark was a lie, of course, but the Fleming did not dare to tell that he had spent a good part of the time drinking, instead of hurrying to Leyden with his precious catch.

"No other exit, you say? Doesn't the chimney of a miserable farmer's room count?"

"Its opening was closed, your reverence, and to prove that I know how to take care of my business, I had several bundles of straw burned underneath the chimney so that the heretic should have fallen down half-choked to death if he had hid himself in there."

"What about the floor, then, couldn't you detect a trap door, or something similar, in it?"

"Nothing, your reverence. The floor consisted of hard clay, covered only by a straw mat. I had this mat removed, but I could not discover anything. And afterwards I searched the entire place, assisted by the helpful housewife and her husband. We searched everything—the stable, the barn, the shed, even the pigpen. But the heretic was gone, and only Satan, whose natural offspring these heretics are, must have delivered him."

Del Castro started to pace the floor impatiently again.

"You just don't know your business, captain, and you don't deserve the confidence I have placed in you. Do you know what I think of the whole thing? That you have allowed yourself to be fooled by the so-called kindness of an ignorant farmer's wife. While you were no doubt drinking, as usual—oh, don't deny it!—those peasants found a way to let the heretic escape. It is exactly their readiness to help you that sounds suspicious to me. There was no better way to keep you away from the place where the heretic was hidden. I still don't understand how you dare face me, having lost such a good catch!"

The captain was struck dumb. He had to admit to himself that the search could have been far more careful if his brain had not been clouded by strong drink; hence he remained standing humbly before the Inquisitor.

Del Castro, realizing that he had touched the captain in his weakest spot, and knowing by which tricks heretics often succeeded in escaping persecution, said in a somewhat softer tone of voice to the Fleming, "I am giving you ten more days to deliver the heretic into my hands. I am leaving here tomorrow. I shall stay in The Hague for four days at the most, where I shall lodge at the home of the priest of St. Jacob's Church. From there I am going to Amsterdam, where you can inquire at the court where I live. And now, depart, and try to erase the shame with which you have covered yourself."

"Would your reverence be so kind as to give me some indications or commands in which direction I should search?" the captain asked.

"Where else than in the neighborhood where you saw the heretic last! No doubt he won't be far away from there and will remain hidden until he thinks that the first storm has passed. Here," Del Castro continued, turning to a beautifully carved chest from which he took several gold coins, "spare no money if this will help you to catch the heretic."

Bowing repeatedly, the captain left the room.

"And now, Cornelio, let us eat, my friend! After you have packed our traveling bag pretty soon, you may go for a walk and pay a visit to the Roman Fort."

7

A Surprising Discovery

As soon as Cornelio had put the numerous documents and other things of his master into the bag, he made use of permission to go out. The weather was not very inviting, to be sure, but since he had been busy writing for most of the day, he considered himself fortunate to be able to get some fresh air.

It had stopped snowing, and the thin white blanket that covered the ground, still frozen hard, was no obstacle for the swift, young feet of the secretary to move fast.

With a large degree of curiosity, peculiar to strangers, he walked through the streets of Leyden which in those days was undoubtedly one of the most prosperous cities in Holland.

Everywhere in the surrounding counties, even as far as in Flanders and northern France, Leyden cloth was renowned, and Leyden brewers contested, not without good reason, the fame attached to Leyden for its Delft beer.

The exterior of the houses in the main streets — although they could hardly be called streets according to our present-day standards, since most of them were not paved — clearly indicated the prosperity of the inhabitants.

With pleasure Cornelio considered the peculiar building style which our forebears followed in the beginning of the sixteenth century. The crow-stepped gables of the red brick houses; the white cornerstones which were inserted between the red brick, and in the form of bands between the different floors or in arches above the windows; the artistically forged anchors that reinforced the gables with their scrolls; the stone-cut corner ornaments; and every now and then the richly carved oakwood awnings — all these things attested not only to the prosperity but also to the taste and artistic sense of the inhabitants.

To be sure, in the streets behind the ramparts and in the many alleys and slums where the weavers usually lived, the houses looked more like pigpens than dwellings of human beings, but Cornelio did not see these at all.

While thus walking, alone and peacefully, something began to stir in the soul of the young priest that had long been dormant. It was the memory of his youth and the environment of his early childhood.

Within the walls of the monastery where he had been taken when twelve years old, he had spent many carefree days, and even more sad ones. Even though a bird may sing in its cage, there are nevertheless moments when its yearning for freedom and the wide skies revives again. Then it beats its wings against the trellis that keeps him imprisoned and flutters restlessly from one perch to the other.

Cornelio had experienced something similar. As lies in the nature of youth, he had soon forgotten the sorrow on account of the loss of his parents when he was with other boys, and only a vague memory of earlier happiness lived on in his soul.

While at the University of Louvain he had had more liberty, but it was a freedom he could hardly enjoy because his studies took all his time. He had not made many friends and kept company only with those who spoke Dutch and who, like him, studied at the famous Louvain school.

He owed it to his great skill with the quill and his knowledge of Dutch that he had been appointed as Del Castro's secretary, and it was now for the first time that he saw Holland again during the few weeks that he had been employed by his master. The memory of his youth became stronger again and the thought that he would be in The Hague by tomorrow caused his heart to beat faster.

There he would try to locate the places where he had played as a boy, and maybe he would see the house again in which his dear mother had died.

A Surprising Discovery

His mother!

In his mind he saw her with the soft, lovely face of the Virgin Mother in the painting that hung in the chapel of the monastery. He remembered how she used to tell him many wonderful stories while he was sitting on a low wooden stool at her knees. How many strange songs she had taught him! And he remembered also that she had taught him to pray in a way that later had been depicted to him as sinful and bad.

Was it the air in Holland or was it the sight of those peculiar houses that sharpened his memory so much? Was it his native soil that caused the words and sounds of his mother to re-echo in his soul?

How often had he tried later, when he grew up, to recall the past during lonely hours or in the stillness of the night and had only partially succeeded! And now the images of the past forced themselves in clear outlines upon him.

Suddenly he remembered the words of a prayer which he had learned at his mother's knee many, many years ago:

> *Behold my agony, oh Lord!*
> *In my affliction strength afford,*
> *Lest I succumb and soon deny Thee.*
> *Oh, keep me faithful to Thy Word*
> *Unto the bitter end if need be!*

And now he also remembered clearly how the superior had called for him after he had sung this song in the garden of the monastery and had threatened to put him on bread and water in a dark cell if he would ever repeat these words. The superior had made him repeat the Hail Mary and the Pater Noster so often until he had finally fallen asleep.

Cornelio once again repeated the words of the song and closely examined them, but could not find anything in them that justified the punishment he had received for singing them when a boy.

His cousin Anne-Bet, who had died a few years ago, had hinted at times that his mother had not been as fervent a Roman Catholic as would have been desirable and knew more of the new doctrine than she could justify, but he could not remember that at all. The song that came into his mind a few minutes ago certainly could not have been composed by heretics! These scoundrels had always been depicted to him in such horrible colors that it would be sacrilegious to ascribe such lovely words to them.

He did not know all the teachings of these heretics, and what little he did know was nothing but a misrepresentation of the new doctrine. Besides, the school he had last attended did not follow the disputes and treatises regarding the doctrines of the Reformation. Only a few times had he been allowed to attend the lectures of Michiels de Bay, dean of St. Peter's Church at Louvain. This doctor of theology, who in the world of education was called Bajus — although he was a bitter enemy of the Reformation — had run into considerable trouble because he himself was by no means orthodox Roman Catholic in every respect. This became quite evident at the Council of Trent.

So Cornelio confidently rejected the idea that his mother might have been a heretic and, humming softly to himself, he continued his walk until he approached the inn, "The Crown."

In those days it was by no means unusual to find someone in religious garb in an inn or tavern with a full glass and a game of dice in front of him or a deck of cards in his hands. On the contrary, especially many members of the lower religious orders and many monks were frequent visitors to such places. For that reason it grieved the pious Roman Catholic burghers to so often see people in religious clothing stumble in a drunken stupor along the road.

Cornelio did not hesitate to enter "The Crown"; he ordered a mug of wine. Nobody in the room seemed to notice the young priest when he entered. Only a portly farmer looked with some interest at the new guest; at least when the owner of the inn passed the man, the farmer asked, "Who is that young man?"

"I don't know, sir," the owner answered. "I think he is a clerk of the Honorable Provincial Inquisitor, who at present is in town here. He certainly is a stranger because all the others"— meaning the other guests in religious garb who regularly visited "The Crown"—"I know and they do not drink wine!"

"But it is strange," mumbled the farmer; "I want to find

A Surprising Discovery

out." It was not long before the countryman, with the jovial boldness characteristic of his class, was engaged in a lively conversation with Cornelio.

"Your speech reveals that you have lived a long time in a foreign country, sir," the farmer remarked inquisitively.

"Yes, sir, indeed I have. I was in Wallonia for over three years, and even though one may remain a good Hollander in his heart, his tongue may nevertheless acquire a foreign twist when one speaks French all the time!" Laughing, Cornelio took a big swallow from the large mug while the farmer looked at him intently. Cornelio noticed that and asked, "Is there something wrong with me?"

"It isn't that but, you see, you look so much like someone I knew real well, especially when you laugh, that I am amazed about it. And I am wondering where I may have seen that face before. Ah! I know! You look exactly like the wife of the cheese merchant from The Hague. I did business with her husband for years until all of a sudden he sold his business. I often visited in the home of the woman, and the more I look at you, the more resemblance I see in your features."

Cornelio was greatly touched.

"What was the name of that cheese merchant?" he asked.

"Well, we always called him simply Harm!"

"My father's name was Harm too, and he was a cheese merchant in the Achterom," Cornelio said.

"But then you must be Harm's son. No doubt about it!" the farmer exclaimed. "Your face is exactly like that of your mother — like two drops of water. The same blond hair and a dimple in the chin! Exactly like your mother!"

"But my mother has been dead a long time!" Cornelio interrupted the farmer as if still doubting whether the man made a mistake.

"Certainly, I know that. The good woman left this vale of tears early, and it has grieved your father not a little to lose your mother."

"My father never knew that my mother had died, so I think that you are mistaken about me, sir. My father perished miserably in the water, according to what I have been told," Cornelio sighed.

Now it was the farmer's turn to look up in disbelief. Could it be possible that this young man did not know what everybody in the Achterom knew?

"Listen, brother," the farmer said after a pause, "what you just said removes every doubt in my heart. You are Harm's son as surely as my name is Jochems. Yes, everybody thought that Harm Hiddesz had perished with the skipper, but"— here the farmer reverently bared his head—"the Lord had something else in store for him. After a long absence he unexpectedly returned and found that his good wife had died. His oldest son had been taken away by a cousin and the youngest child was being cared for by a neighbor. From grief your father discontinued his business and started to wander from one place to another. Every now and then he returned to visit his youngest son and when the child was about six years old, I believe, he left with him and he has not been seen in The Hague since."

Speechless, and with bated breath, Cornelio had listened to the short story of the farmer. With his tightly clenched right hand he tried to subdue the wild beating of his heart. At last he exploded. He stood up and placed his hand on the farmer's shoulder and said, "Man, don't deceive me! Is it the truth what you just said? Has my father not drowned then? My father is *alive*?"

The farmer looked at Cornelio again. He seemed to hesitate before answering him.

"Say something!" Cornelio cried.

"Whether your father is still living is known only to the Lord, but if you want a confirmation of my story, then go to The Hague and ask for the cobbler's wife who lives in the Achterom. She will probably be able to tell you more than I can."

The farmer arose from his seat and departed. Cornelio, who had slumped back on his bench, did not even notice that the man had left.

Deep in thought and shaking his head, the farmer continued his walk. "Marvelous are Thy ways, great God," he softly said, "and who can fathom Thy doings?"

When Cornelio got home, his first thought was to tell his master and confidant Del Castro what he had learned so unexpectedly. With his great influence and the means at his disposal, it would not be difficult for Del Castro to search in

A Surprising Discovery 61

the direction indicated by the farmer for Cornelio's father and to clarify the dark mystery that surrounded this whole matter.

But to the clerk's great disappointment, the Provincial Inquisitor had gone out in order to discuss important matters with several members of the city council and the higher clergy of Leyden, and he came home so late that night that Cornelio decided to wait until the next day. So he went to bed, but no matter how he turned and tossed, could not get to sleep. Again and again the story of the farmer came back to his mind and the questions multiplied.

Could that farmer have been mistaken and was he, Cornelio, therefore entertaining false hopes? But that was almost impossible. That man had told him that everyone in the neighborhood where his father had lived knew that he had not drowned. Had he not mentioned the shoemaker's wife to whom his little brother — he hardly remembered the child anymore — had been taken and had lived there until his father himself had come to get him?

But what was the reason, then, that this father had absolutely never made any attempts to get in contact with his elder son? Had he not always shown that he loved his oldest child? How tender always had been his embrace when he returned from his trips and Cornelio ran to meet him! Then he would lift him high up in the air with a face that beamed with joy! And every time his father had been away from home, he always had brought something pretty or pleasant for his Hidde, as he was called before he had donned the clerical garb.

And this father was supposed to be alive and yet never to have looked for his child? He had never asked where his son could be? Cornelio became more and more confused by all these questions that arose in his mind.

If he had understood the farmer correctly, then that little brother who was a mere infant when his dear mother died was still living too. But he, Cornelio, himself had asked the superior of the monastery where he was reared what had become of that child, and the superior, as well as old Anne-Bet, had told him for certain that the child had died soon after the death of his mother.

If all the inhabitants of the Achterom, as the farmer had

assured him, had known his father afterwards and had seen that child grow up to boyhood, how could it be explained that his superiors had kept the truth from him? Was he to conclude then that they had lied to him? He hesitated to formulate this suspicion in his own mind. And yet, he could not suppress this thought. Why should they have behaved like that? In order to get hold of his parents' possessions? Indeed, what had become of these possessions? Anne-Bet had said that she had regulated and taken care of all these things. That was why he had received an education which now placed him in a higher position than that of other householders' sons.

"Considering everything," Cornelio thought, "here is a mystery that is difficult to fathom and the motives of which may forever remain secret."

But if his spiritual fathers were anxious to keep this secret from him — and Cornelio already knew to what length they sometimes could go in such matters — then it would be foolish for him to ask Del Castro for a solution, no matter how kindly disposed he was towards him in other respects. Then it would be far better for him to keep his eyes open and to try to find out for himself until he had solved this dark mystery.

When the sun arose, Cornelio was still deeply absorbed in thought. But the Inquisitor's secretary greeted the new day with joy too, because within a couple of hours he would again see the city where he was born — after so many years. Not only would he see it back again, but there he would, as he fervently hoped, receive from the lips of eyewitnesses, of old neighbors and acquaintances, some indications that would help him find his father again.

8

The Escape

While Cornelio accompanies his master Del Castro to The Hague, we return to the home of Hannes the farmer and continue our interrupted story from the moment when Harm Hiddesz was bound and locked up in the dark room.

There we find the faithful witness of the truth with his hands tied to his back and not knowing where they would take him but fully realizing his precarious situation.

He knew that for the last couple of years his activity as a preacher of the divine Word had drawn the attention of the persecutors of the Reformation. His name was listed in the books of the Inquisition as one of the heretics whose capture was greatly desired.

More than once already he had miraculously escaped from his persecutors, and several people — often those of whom he expected it least of all — had given him a safe hiding place in spite of the fact that the placards threatened with the death penalty every person who gave shelter to heretics.

Nevertheless, Harm Hiddesz had never flattered himself with the thought that he would not, as so many before him had been, be called upon to seal the preaching of the doctrine of free grace with his life. Such an "offering" of his body he considered as nothing compared with the great blessings which Christ had merited for him. Like all the martyrs before the throne of the Lamb, he too would gladly lay his head on the scaffold or be bound to the stake, wishing only that his heavenly Father would keep him faithful when facing his persecutors so that he might keep that which had been committed to his trust.

But for all his courage, which was the result of a conviction that had been wrought by the Holy Spirit, and for all the zeal for the honor of his crucified King, Harm Hiddesz at the same time felt the power of the ties of blood that still bound his flesh to the earth.

A little distance away there lay the sick lad, the only child that had been left him from a pure and happy marriage. There lay the child among completely strange people who maybe tomorrow, like himself, could get into the greatest difficulties for the sake of the truth. How he would have liked to stay at the bedside of his Adriaan, to comfort him, to take care of him, to nurse him like a mother would!

To be sure, Harm Hiddesz knew the promise that his covenant God would be a Father also to this orphan; but even the most assured Christian knows by experience that although the spirit is willing, the flesh may be weak, and that it can be a bitter ordeal for the soul to part submissively from the dearest loved ones.

And now the father would not even be able to say goodbye to his child; he would not be allowed to press a kiss on that dear forehead burning with fever. Oh, how Harm wished that he could kneel once more at the child's bedside to commit him, in a final embrace, into the hands of his faithful God!

It did not enter his mind that this time there again might be a possibility of escape. It seemed obvious to him that the woman, in order to save the child from the persecutors, had surrendered the father into their hands.

Oh, if the lad only did not call for him! His heart tightened with fear at the thought that the joking, noisy soldiers might notice the presence of the little fellow. This fear overwhelmed him to such an extent that he longed for the moment that they would come and take him away.

But in the other room they did not think of leaving. In his great fear Harm Hiddesz listened whether he could hear Adriaan's voice. Motionless he stood in the middle of the dark room.

Then he suddenly heard a creaking sound. Or was he mistaken? No, there it was again, clearer than before; a creaking, dragging sound. But it did not come from where the farmer's wife was seated. The darkness prevented him from seeing what the cause of this unusual noise could be. He cocked his ears, but then it was quiet again. But only for a moment. There he heard it again. It seemed as if the wall to the right of him was being moved out of its joints.

Then the thought of rescue suddenly flitted as a beam of light into his soul. No doubt about it! An attempt was being made there to make a way of escape for him! His heart started to beat faster.

Did the faithful God of Jacob want to keep him from death again and was He sending him a liberating angel? And who could that be? Were they not all together in the other room?

Harm Hiddesz did not know that one person was missing in that company. And that one person was Bouke, the deformed Bouke!

Hannes's wife had spoken only a few hurried words to him in the cowstable, but Bouke had understood what they meant. With a key which the farmer's wife had pressed into his hand he had entered the dark, narrow hall that led to the front door of the house, the door that was always locked.

Carefully, almost inaudibly, he turned the old rusty lock, and opened a door which in earlier days used to give entrance to Mrs. Hannes's best room. But entering the room was not easy because the large oakwood cabinet which contained an abundance of linen, mostly spun and woven by the farmer's wife herself, stood in front of that door and covered its opening completely. And there was no one to help Bouke move this terribly heavy piece of furniture! If Bouke could only move it far enough for him to get his hand through the crack, then master Harm would be saved. So Bouke tried to shove the cabinet forward, but the heavy piece seemed to mock his phenomenal strength. Must that faithful servant of the Lord then become the prey of his persecutors and soon perish at the hand of an executioner?

Bouke looked around in despair. Heavy drops of sweat ran through the deep grooves of his deformed face. Once more he tried to shove the awkward chest from its place. With all the strength he could muster he tried to squeeze his body between the cabinet and the wall. The chest started to creak and moved slightly. With clenched teeth and every muscle of his crooked body flexed, and holding his breath, Bouke continued to press. Only a few more inches to go — and the faithful servant grabbed Harm Hiddesz in the dark. A few seconds later the leather straps that bound his hands were cut loose.

Neither of the two men spoke a word. Holding Bouke's hand, Harm followed him and squeezed himself through the narrow opening and into the hall. Together they pulled the cabinet with all their strength back and after a few moments it looked as if it had never been from its place.

After having locked the door carefully, Bouke, holding the hand of the preacher, led him away. He intended to hide Harm Hiddesz under the hay above the cowstable.

But time had run out. In the living room the captain had gotten up from his chair, and Bouke noticed by the cursing and terrible noise inside, that he had put the chest back in place and shut the door not a second too early. There was no longer time to hide Harm above the cowstable. The soldiers would open the door that gave entrance to the front room and would find him with the fugitive.

The farmhand looked around in the darkness as though he could clearly discern every object in the front room. He quickly lifted the lid from the large milk vat that stood beside the cooling trough — the vat that the day before had been full to the brim but which now was completely empty.

With a few words he indicated to Harm Hiddesz that this was the place for him to hide himself. Without hesitation Harm jumped into the barrel which was large enough to hold two persons. Then Bouke nonchalantly put the lid back on the vat which now held such a precious load. As though nothing had happened, he took the lantern from its hook in the wall so that when the captain, followed by his henchmen and the farmer's family, opened the door, it looked for all the world as if Bouke had just lighted the lantern to guide the soldiers outside.

With his one good eye half closed, and yawning fearfully, he approached the captain. "Are the gentlemen leaving?" he asked, still yawning.

The Escape

"No, you impudent lout!" the captain snapped. "You are going to light the way for us. And we are not going to leave until we have that heretic back again."

As obedient as a dog, Bouke led the captain into every nook and cranny in the stable and in the pigpen and through the barn and the cellar. What the result of this search was we already learned from the account the captain gave Del Castro, the Provincial Inquisitor.

9

How Harm Hiddesz Was Saved

No matter how they hunted and searched, the heretic was nowhere to be found. Three or four times the captain brushed past the vat in which Harm was huddled, who with trembling heart and silently praying to God was awaiting the outcome.

Once the Fleming struck the barrel with his sword, but it had not occurred to the captain or to any of his half-drunk companions to lift up the lid.

Cursing and swearing, they departed at last, fully convinced that Satan himself must have carried the heretic off. Bouke accompanied them a short distance, carrying his lantern. They returned to the ferryhouse where miserly Aart was waiting for his reward.

Bouke stood there watching them for a while, and when he felt that the three soldiers were far enough away, he hurried back to the farmhouse.

Harm Hiddesz had not dared to come out of hiding as yet, so when Bouke entered the house he found the woman and Hannes and Melis impatiently awaiting his return.

"Where is master Harm?" all three asked him at the same time. Triumphantly Bouke walked ahead of them and led them to the front room. There he lifted the lid from the vat and the others saw to their utter amazement Harm Hiddesz appear. He looked pale and somewhat shaken. Even the woman had not suspected that master Harm had been that close.

"The Lord be praised!" she cried, deeply moved.

"Amen!" the two farmers said, reverently uncovering their heads.

Harm Hiddesz, however, walked up to Bouke who, modestly and with a blank expression on his face as though what he had done were the simplest thing in the world, stood in the background.

Harm Hiddesz placed his left hand on the shoulder of the deformed little fellow and raising his right hand as if appealing to the Almighty to be his witness, he solemnly and with trembling voice said, "May the Lord reward you, Bouke, for what you have done for one of the least of His servants! May He, according to His promise, give you a thousandfold reward of grace. And may you in the Day of days hear from the mouth of the King of glory: 'Verily I say unto you, Inasmuch as you have done this unto one of the least of these my brethren, you have done it unto me'!"

Bouke, the giant in the shape of a dwarf, trembled with emotion. In Hannes he had found a kind master, and the farmer's wife had ever been like a sister to him. But in the world outside he was often the butt of the silly jokes of the peasants, an object of scorn and mockery. Already in his youth life seemed not worth living to him, and often his heart was filled with bitter anger and hatred towards his tormentors. Then his soul would rebel against God and he would ask himself: "Why must I drag such a despicable body around while everybody else enjoys well-formed limbs? Why did I, as a reward for my sacrifice in saving my master's possessions, have to be deformed in my face for life as if I were not hideous enough already?"

That was long ago now, for when he had learned to search for the Lord and grace had been glorified in his heart, his attitude had changed; he had learned to bear the mockery of the world when he considered the shame and the cross of his Lord. Until now, however, no one had ever addressed him the way Harm Hiddesz had just done. And he resolved that from now on he would even give his life for this brother, if need be!

Returning to the living room, where the crocks and mugs still testified to the carousal of the soldiers, Harm Hiddesz and his friends knelt down in prayer. Once again master Harm could praise the faithfulness of his Lord and King; he could testify of the secret place of the Most High and the shadow of the Almighty. A sweet incense rose up in the name of Jesus Christ to the God of Jacob who is a fortress for His people; and with renewed faith the fellow brethren in tribulation, indeed, the whole church militant was remembered in intercessory prayer before her glorified Head in heaven.

Harm Hiddesz would have loved to continue the discussion of God's marvelous deeds, but his fatherly heart drew him to the bedstead of his Adriaan.

The lad uttered a shout of joy when his father entered the little alcove, and with tears of joy Harm Hiddesz embraced his son and pressed him to his heart.

"Oh Father!" the boy said, his cheeks and eyes burning with fever, "how glad I am that those cursing soldiers have left. I heard that they were talking about you, and I knew that they wanted to take you away, because Job, the old fisherman, has told me many stories about men and women and also children who were killed because they loved the Lord and His Word. That's why I kept very quiet, so that they wouldn't find me too; and I kept softly praying to the Lord that they would not take you away." While saying this, he kissed the face of his father.

"And the Lord Jesus heard your prayer, my child," Harm Hiddesz replied. "It pleases Him to let your father stay with you a while longer yet. And now, my Adriaan, try to go to sleep now, and remember that the Lord sends His angels to watch over us so that no harm can befall us. I shall wet this cloth around your head first because you still have a fever. I have to discuss a few things with these good people in the other room. After that I shall come back again."

The boy let his father take care of him and then laid his head down on the pillow.

Harm Hiddesz returned to Hannes and his wife to discuss what he should do next. When several people have to discuss a serious matter, they often express different opinions and propose varying courses of action. This was also the case here.

Harm Hiddesz himself had not made any plans yet, as he wanted to hear first what his host and his wife thought should be done.

Hannes proposed to take Harm in his wagon to Rotterdam early the next morning; from there he could go to the fisherman in Zeeland, where it would be safer for him to stay than on the farm. Melis thought that the city offered better opportunities to hide, because many friends and brethren lived there, and if the Inquisition should discover his whereabouts, his chance to escape was far greater there than on a lonely farm where everybody could see from a great distance when a person entered or left the house.

Bouke, whose opinion was also solicited, wanted to hide Harm Hiddesz in the haystack for the time being.

"And what is the opinion of the good woman?" Harm Hiddesz asked.

"A plan as to how to get from here to a safer place I do not have," the farmer's wife replied. "But," she continued, "we had better consider whether it is wise to be in such a hurry to get away from here. Most likely they are thinking that you are hurrying away to find a safe place, and it seems to me that for a while they will not return to our house to look for you here. It is important, however, that we keep you out of sight of curious people who undoubtedly will come here in order to hear a little more from us regarding the escaped heretic. You can be sure that those half-drunk soldiers have been talking in the ferryhouse, and when the ferryman hears some news, then in one day it will be known everywhere, from the Rhine dike to the Dam. If you stay in hiding during the day — which is not difficult — then, it seems to me, you could stay here for some time until tonight's events have been somewhat forgotten. If the little one may recover soon, I believe that the two of you could go to Rotterdam more easily when you travel at night."

"But, my dear wife," Hannes interrupted here, "you forget that it is mid-winter right now. How can you insist that master Harm and his boy travel at night?"

"I should think," the woman continued, "that we must choose the lesser of two evils. We have many friends here in the neighborhood. If the ice stays good, Melis or Bouke can take master Harm and the little one, warmly covered in the sleigh, quite a distance away; for example, to Krelis van Dieren. Master Harm could stay there during the day and Krelis could take him to another friend; and I dare say that this way, by going through the polders and staying away from the roads, he could readily reach Rotterdam. The farther away from here the less the chance that people will recognize or apprehend him. At any rate, master Harm will have to wait until the child is better, unless he wants to go alone. I shall be happy to take care of the lad if his father is willing to entrust him to my care."

Harm Hiddesz remained silent and in thought for some time. First of all he concluded that his going to the old fisherman would not be in the interest of the cause of the gospel to which he felt called, for staying with that brother, no matter how pleasant their fellowship would be, would force him into inactivity. For the next weeks or maybe even months there would be very little he could do in Holland and Zeeland, which were his appointed fields of labor. As long as Del Castro, the Provincial Inquisitor, with his large staff of spies and persecutors, traveled all over Holland, unrestrained activity on his own part would at the same time increase the danger for the brethren. In other parts of the Netherlands there were preachers of the Reformation; for during the last couple of years the churches in the German Rhine provinces, which had accepted the Reformation and which allowed the adherents of the new doctrine a certain measure of liberty, had concerned themselves with the cause of the Dutch brethren. These churches had sent ordained ministers to the areas. It is true, they were not preachers who had studied at the Roman Catholic universities; nevertheless, neither were they men who were wholly unprepared to take up the difficult task of spreading the gospel among subjects of a tyrannical government.

It was imperative that Harm Hiddesz, if he wished to remain faithful to his calling, be not restricted in his activities on account of the boy for whose safety and future he was responsible as father. Since it seemed to him that the woman's judgment was correct, and his persecutors would not come and search for him on the farm for the next few days, Harm Hiddesz decided not to leave right away but to wait a while until Adriaan's condition would no longer prevent him from traveling. So he informed his hospitable friends of his decision and they immediately accepted it.

10

A Blessed Deathbed

A few days passed without the peace on the farm being disturbed. Nevertheless, the people there were not without great concern, which was caused by an unexpected happening. One morning when Bouke got up he was not, as usual, greeted by the happy barking of the watchdog. He immediately suspected foul play and started to hunt around the farm buildings, calling the dog's name as he went. Soon he found the faithful animal some distance from the farm, dead from apparent poisoning.

Harm Hiddesz immediately suspected danger. The death of the dog was obviously the result of evil intentions and unmistakably justified his fear that the farm was surrounded by spies who had succeeded in getting rid of the watchful dog.

From that moment the people on the farm moved with extreme caution, and only at night when the blinds were shut would master Harm come out of hiding and spend a few hours amid the family circle to eat supper together and to end the day with reading and praying together.

The hours thus spent were often hours of spiritual joy, since it could be truly said that the Lord was manifestly in their midst; but sometimes these hours were also spent in anxious discussions when a cloud of fear and downheartedness hung over the small band and their hearts were filled with apprehension. Then their eye of faith could hardly penetrate the mists and it was difficult for them to cast their anchor of faith behind the veil. Then they thoroughly discussed every possibility of escape once more. Every little event that had taken place during the day was carefully scrutinized.

During the day Harm Hiddesz remained, as had been agreed upon, in the little alcove with his son, and there they were supplied with every need by the kindhearted farmer's wife.

Whenever a visitor appeared unexpectedly, even the most observing stranger could not have discovered anything out of the ordinary in the household of farmer Hannes; and it was exactly as the woman had expected — many a visitor knocked at the door of the farmhouse. Every time Mrs. Hannes had to give an extensive account of the inexplicable escape of the heretic, and every time a farmer or a farmer's wife stopped in, the woman had to open the door to the best room and show the place where the heretic had been locked up. Many a visitor left shaking his head in astonishment.

Soon the curiosity of the people wore off. There was only one person from the neighborhood who came to visit the farm more often than he ever had done before, and every time he came back to the same subject, namely, the escape of the heretic.

"What that miserly Aart has up his sleeve lately I don't know," the woman had often thought to herself. "In the past we saw him seldom or never and now he shows up every moment, or else wanders around in the neighborhood of the farm. There must be something behind all this!"

As far as Harm Hiddesz was concerned, he yearned to leave. In the cottage of Job the fisherman he would be safer than anywhere else. At some distance from the fisherman's dwelling was a little boat. That would leave no tracks on the Zeeland waters when it was being driven by powerful oars or the wind.

But leaving now was out of the question. Instead of getting better, Adriaan's condition worsened by the day. His fevers increased in frequency and intensity and the boy was obviously losing ground. And when sometimes in the middle of the night the lad with a shout would rise up to escape the persecutors he saw in his feverish imagination, Harm Hiddesz would take his son into his arms but the boy would still keep on crying, "Father, Father!" and would try to free himself from his father's embrace. When Harm Hiddesz in the silence of the night stood powerless over against the destroyer who drained the last strength of his darling, a desperate cry escaped his bleeding heart. Then he pleaded with his God and wrestled with the Lord like Jacob did at the ford of Jabbok. Then Harm Hiddesz referred to the eternal promises, which are yea and amen, and he could not refrain from beseeching God to spare his Benjamin, the only son left to him.

In this regard too, however, Harm had to experience that the ways of the God's unfathomable wisdom often lead through deep places. The usually strong man had to learn to realize his utter weakness and experience that the willing surrender of the dearest loved one cannot be accomplished by flesh and blood. He had to be loosed from much that still bound him to this earth so that he could unreservedly and wholeheartedly dedicate himself to the work of Him who had called him to labor in His vineyard.

When Adriaan's illness took such an alarming turn, the men discussed with Mrs. Hannes whether it were possible to send for a physician. Hannes said that in Leyden there were some monks who were renowned for their knowledge of medicines; but it was impossible under the circumstances Harm found himself in to invite a priest to the house.

"If the old chaplain of Duivenvoorde Castle were still living," the woman said, "I would have gone over there to get some good medicine a long time ago, and I would not even have been afraid to let him come over here."

Melis remembered that in Leyden there lived an old man who was very much in demand by the common people for his medicines. Maybe he could be prevailed upon to come and see the lad. Immediately the robust farmer went on his way.

On the towing path along the Vliet he met miserly Aart, who also seemed to be in a hurry to get to Leyden, and Melis was half obliged to accompany him. Although both asked the other where he was going and for what reason, both understood that the other gave an evasive answer in order to keep the real purpose a secret.

As Melis had feared, the old man was too weak to accompany him to the farm; but he gave Melis an extract from some herbs to take along to the boy, which might help the fever to dimish or disappear.

Happy that he could take home such valuable medicine, as he believed, Melis hurried back, and since he had had to wait rather long for the extract to be prepared, it was almost dark when he returned to the farm.

But what a change he found there! His sister and brother-in-law and Bouke stood beside Harm Hiddesz around the bed of the lad. He could read a deep emotion on the faces of these people, an emotion that grips even the most indifferent person when death spreads its dark wings over the bedstead of a sick one. Even in Bouke's face something quivered which lent to his deformed features a soft, tender expression. Mrs. Hannes lifted every now and then a corner of her apron to her eyes and wiped away some tears.

Harm Hiddesz stood motionless and with folded hands, and while his heart tightened with grief, he saw the breathing of the boy become shorter and shorter. He saw how the lad turned his head from one side to the other and now and then pressed a tightly closed hand on his chest to curb the wild beating of the young heart.

How different things had looked that morning, and how well the lad had seemed! Or had Harm Hiddesz failed to see that that brightness of spirit, that great desire to speak, had been the symptoms that betrayed the approaching end?

"Dear Father!" Adriaan had asked, "are you reading from Mother's Bible?"

"Yes, son. Do you want me to read something to you?"

"Yes, Father!"

"What do you want me to read to you?"

"Oh, please read about the City with the twelve gates of pearl and the streets of gold, about the heavenly Jerusalem where the redeemed ever sing of God's mercy. Read about the throne in which the Lord Jesus sits, and about the saints who are standing before the throne in their long white robes with their palm branches in their hands."

A Blessed Deathbed

The boy's eyes had glistened when he had spoken these words, but in the dark corner of the little alcove Harm Hiddesz had not noticed that. So the father opened the little Bible again and read from the Revelation of John about the New City, and with the eye of faith he for a moment beheld the glory of that house with the many mansions where Jesus had gone to prepare a place for all His own, both great and small.

And Adriaan? This twelve-year-old lad who on account of not having been much around boys of his own age had retained much of his childlike innocence and yet, through the talks of the God-fearing fisherman, was so much ahead of many children his age in knowledge and deeper insight. Adriaan too, enlightened by the Spirit who had worked in his heart already at an early age, had seen the City of Life. But, being close to its gate, he saw it far more clearly than his father.

The boy's spirit began to make itself loose from the flesh; the butterfly began to extricate itself from the cocoon which prevented it from unfolding its wings.

"Adriaan," Harm Hiddesz said when he had finished reading, "you are very sick, and although I have prayed to the Lord Jesus every day that you might get better, it appears to me that you are going to die. If that is so, are you not afraid? You know very well, don't you, that not all who depart from here will arrive in this New City?"

When his father mentioned the word "die" a small, almost unnoticeable quiver crossed Adriaan's face, but this lasted only a second and he quickly controlled his emotions. The new life which he would continue eternally in endless bliss drew him stronger than natural life.

"Afraid, dear Father?" he asked. "No, I know that Jesus my Redeemer lives, and soon I shall see Him face to face."

"Adriaan! Do you know what you are saying?" his father cried out, deeply moved and yet with holy joy.

"Certainly, dear Father, for when I did not think of Him nor asked for Him, the Lord Jesus came to me and said, 'My son, give me your heart.' And I know only too well how unwilling I was to give Him my whole heart. But then He took it, in spite of my tears, and I learned to love Him, much more and in an entirely different way than I love you. And now I know that I will be where He is! When you go back to Job he will tell you more about it."

Harm Hiddesz had wept when he heard these words and, all the while weeping, he had taken his child into his arms. The tears that rolled down the cheeks of the preacher had not been tears of grief but of joy and, fully surrendered, he had whispered: "If it is Thy will, Lord, then take also the last possession I have here on earth. I willingly surrender it to Thee. Let my child be praising Thee in heaven while I, struggling and sorrowing, continue the way which Thou wilt show me here below."

At noon the fever had become worse. Like the howling wind tosses the slender craft to and fro on the heaving waves, so the fever wasted the boy's body. And now that the fever decreased, the lad's heart began to beat more slowly. Harm Hiddesz had called the farmer's wife and she called her husband and Bouke, because the boy was dying. And that is how Melis found them, all gathered around Adriaan's bed.

"Father!" the boy cried, and looked searchingly around.

"Here I am, my son; what is it you want?"

"When I shall see my mother and little sister in heaven, what shall I tell them?"

"Oh my child, my child!" the father sobbed. "Tell them," he said while the tears streamed down his cheeks, "tell them that I am greatly desirous to depart and to be with Christ and them, but not before I have run the course which God has appointed for me."

The breathing of the boy became increasingly shorter.

"Father, it is so dark! Where are you?"

Harm Hiddesz took the lad, who had gotten up in a sitting position, into his arms and the boy laid his head against his father's chest.

"Father," Adriaan said haltingly and with gasping intervals, "when you find Hidde, my big brother — and you *will* find him — then tell him that Mother and I shall be waiting for him in heaven," and he pointed upwards. "Tell him that I loved him and often prayed for him, although I never saw him, but that I hope to find him and see him in heaven."

A Blessed Deathbed

Harm Hiddesz no longer wept. Why did this dying child have to rip open that old wound? Or did the Lord wish to renew His promise by the mouth of his youngest darling that he would see his oldest, lost son, back again?

"I shall give your message to Hidde," Harm Hiddesz sighed and kissed the moist forehead of the dying lad.

"Oh, Father dear, how light it is getting! Oh, how beautiful, how glorious!"

The shining eyes dimmed, the exulting mouth stiffened, the tired heart stopped beating, and the angels carried the young lad's soul on rapid wings to the City which he had seen from afar!

Harm Hiddesz did not weep. Indeed, it looked far more like a joyful smile spread over his face. He had seen his child depart into the light of eternal life; and the little sufferer was now there where there is no sorrow, no temptation, no sin, but only holiness and joy before the throne of the Lamb!

No persecutor could stretch out his hand for him anymore; no cruel fanatic could any longer pursue him; no fear could clutch his heart anymore; he was safe — safe in Jesus' arms, safe on Jesus' breast.

Harm Hiddesz silently shouted for joy. In a gesture of thanksgiving he lifted up his arms, as though the greatest benefit had been bestowed upon him; and no one who would have seen him at that moment would have suspected that only a few moments ago his darling had been taken away from him.

Then suddenly, Harm Hiddesz felt a hand on his shoulder, and at the same time the woman and the farmers shrank back.

"This time you won't get away from us!" a voice shouted triumphantly. It was the Fleming, the captain who, unnoticed, had approached the farm and entered the room with his men. In a matter of seconds Harm Hiddesz was surrounded by the armed gang.

The persecuted "heretic" gave no sign of surprise. The death of Adriaan had made such a tremendous impression on his soul that he seemed to be oblivious to any other happening.

With a regal gesture he brushed away the hand which the Fleming had placed on his shoulder and walked over to the bed. "Sleep in peace, my darling," he softly said, closing the lad's eyes which dully stared straight upward. "Sleep in peace, my darling, until the time that also you from this your flesh will behold Him who loved you from all eternity!

"And now, oh Father who art in heaven, Thy will be done!"

Then Harm stretched out his hands to the soldiers who shackled them and, without giving him the opportunity to say a few words to Hannes or his wife, roughly dragged him away.

"With you we'll settle later!" the Fleming snarled at Hannes on his way out.

The captain, whose self-respect had been deeply hurt by the reprimands of the Inquisitor, Del Castro, had determined to prove that he did not carry the name of "heretic hunter" for nothing. In consultation with Antonio, this time he had made his plans far more carefully and shrewdly than the first time. He realized that it would be foolish for him to go to the farm himself to find out whether the heretic was hiding there. When further reflecting on this matter, he had to admit that Del Castro was correct in assuming that the heretic would not dare to show himself in public for the time being. So the Fleming concentrated on a way to learn what transpired in Hannes's house. After much thinking he thought that he had found a way, and already the next day after he had told the Inquisitor about his unsuccessful catch, he was back at the ferryman's.

The ferryman, however, did not appreciate the captain's reappearance very much because he remembered only too well how the man had raged and ranted after he returned unsuccessfully from Hannes's farm. But this time he was just as calm and polite as he had been crude then. At the Fleming's urgent request the ferryman had to show him the way to miserly Aart's place. Aart, who was not only very greedy but also very cowardly by nature, was very much upset when the Fleming appeared at the gate of his farm, but soon the friendly tone of the captain's voice put him at ease.

"In my chagrin and regret on account of the accursed heretic's escape, I completely forgot, my good man, to give you your reward for your willingness to show us the way to the farm," the Fleming said to Aart while he pressed a golden coin in his hand.

The sight of the glittering coin changed Aart completely and at once he led the Fleming into his house and invited him to

A Blessed Deathbed

take a seat near the hearth. That was what the Fleming wanted, and soon the two men were engaged in a confidential conversation.

As the Fleming left, he rubbed his hands with satisfaction. "When a person has no sense of honor, you must work on his greediness," he said when he slowly returned to Leyden. "I believe I have found the right man for this job, for this greedy farmer would sell his own father and mother for a few gold pieces."

And Aart, anxious to earn the money that was promised him, had left no stone unturned to find out what Hannes was doing. When this did not make him much wiser, however, and when all his sly questioning did not help him, he then prowled around, night after night, on the farm, peeking in at the cracks of shutters and doors, to see if he could detect a sign of the heretic. In order to make this possible, he had poisoned the dog, in which, as we already know, he had succeeded only too well. At long last, after having prowled around Hannes's house many a night, one evening he saw by the light of a candle in the living room a stranger. There was no mistake about it, that had to be the heretic; and he would have liked to go to Leyden that same night to tell about his discovery if the late hour had not prevented him from doing so.

But the heretic, he told himself, would not slip through his fingers. The next day, at the same time when Melis left for Leyden to find help for the sick boy, Aart went to see the Fleming there.

The captain wanted to go to the farm at once, but Antonio insisted they wait until dusk in order to enter the farmhouse suddenly, and unnoticed. We have already seen that this plan succeeded perfectly.

The Fleming, followed by Antonio and assisted by two soldiers, carried off Harm Hiddesz, who offered no resistance and who only now and then turned his head to the farm where he had left Adriaan behind whom he would never see again on this earth.

Slowly the men plodded through the heavy snow that covered the earth like a shroud. When they had covered more than half the distance between the farm and the ferryhouse,

Harm turned his head once more. Then he saw a figure that seemed to follow the group, although it kept itself out of sight behind the brush that grew along the path.

The Fleming, too, seemed to have noticed it, because after having commanded Antonio and his men to proceed, he turned around and walked over to the figure which now stopped as if undecided what to do. It was Bouke who, while the others had remained in the house as if crushed, had followed Harm Hiddesz to find out in which direction the prisoner was being transported. Bouke had apparently figured on a long trip because he carried the heavy gnarly stick in his hand with which usually the cows were driven to the market.

"What's the meaning of this?" the Fleming shouted at Bouke. But Bouke did not answer.

"Speak up, you monster! Why are you following us so closely at our heels? Are you an ambassador of Satan trying to snatch the heretic away from us again?" Saying this he walked threateningly over to Bouke.

Bouke remained where he was, but inside of him something started to seethe and boil. He had learned to love Harm Hiddesz; he had seen him standing at the deathbed of his child; he had witnessed the cruelty of these hangman's assistants who dragged the father away from his child's deathbed as if he were the greatest criminal. Now a feeling of deep sorrow — because they were carrying away the man whom he had saved the first time from the hands of the persecutors — added to the indignation that was already filling his heart. And now that cursing captain taunted him! So when the captain stretched out his hand toward Bouke, the latter grabbed the Fleming who was wholly unprepared for this attack, although it was senseless and useless on Bouke's part. But the soldier, when he approached the farmhand, had not thought it necessary to draw his sword out of its sheath, as the thought of an attack from the dwarf did not occur to him.

But this dwarf possessed the strength of a giant. With iron arms he clasped the neck of the Fleming who, being also impeded by his wide mantle, tried to wrest himself free from the choking embrace. It seemed that an anger that had been suppressed for years suddenly awoke inside the dwarf and that

A Blessed Deathbed

in the person of the Fleming he wished to strike all the persecutors of God's children.

With the strength of a Hercules he lifted the captain, his adversary, from the ground and the next moment was rolling with him in the snow. There the fight between the dwarf and the giant continued. It was a battle of life and death.

The Fleming, who had finally succeeded in getting his left arm free, grabbed Bouke's chest and tried to fling him away. But Bouke held on the more tightly, and when the captain let go of the dwarf for a minute to get the broad knife from the sheath on his leather belt with the one hand he had freed to be able to use, Bouke grabbed the Fleming by the throat. His big iron fists cut off the soldier's breath. The man turned over and over in agony of death; it seemed as if the dwarf's body had grown one with his. Snow attached itself to the Fleming's hair; his eyes bulged out of their sockets; his veins stood out like ropes on his forehead! But the farmhand continued clasping the neck of the nearly suffocated heretic hunter.

Had Harm Hiddesz witnessed this struggle, he would have called out to Bouke: "Let go of him! 'Vengeance is mine; I will repay, saith the Lord!'"

Only a few seconds more and the Fleming would have succumbed under the steel grip of the farmhand. Then Bouke suddenly let go and, without uttering a sound, lay still and limp, as if dead. It was Antonio who, wondering what took his master so long, had retraced his steps and witnessed already from a distance the hopeless battle. As soon as he could he had run to the aid of his captain, and had let the knob of his sword come down on Bouke's head so that he had lost consciousness immediately.

Once he was free, the captain pulled himself together again in no time. "I believe that I got here just in time," Antonio, the Spaniard, said with a hint of sarcasm in his voice.

"Well, this accursed dog flew at my throat like a wild animal and I must admit that he has strength in his arms. I hope that you have knocked him out for good."

"I am sure I have! For such vermin my precious sword is too good. I believe that I have killed him with the knob." With an air of disdain he kicked the body of the farmhand who gave no sign of life.

"But let us hurry!" he said. "Over there the heretic might get ideas to play the same tricks."

The two soldiers hurried to catch up with Harm Hiddesz and his keepers.

Bouke remained motionless at the side of the road, his blood gushing from a gaping wound in his skull.

11

An Important Dinner Conversation

The priest of the St. Jacob's parish in The Hague was giving a magnificent dinner. His guest of honor, the Provincial Inquisitor, Del Castro, was going to leave the following day and for that reason the priest from the Warande had invited several members of the city council as well as the most important priests to a farewell dinner.

Following the custom of the Brussels court, the guests had been invited to arrive at a later hour than that at which the evening meal usually was held. Hence they found the large room to which the priest had invited them beautifully illuminated, since darkness fell early at this time of the year. The silver chandeliers spread a bright light in the usually somber room with its dark brown oak paneling. A pile of burning beech logs in the very large hearth spread a pleasant heat. The long table, covered with snow-white Flemish linen, displayed the best fruit from the hothouses in the priest's garden. It was indeed a distinguished company that gathered around this table!

Naturally, the seat of honor was occupied by the celebrated guest whom the priest of St. Jacob's wanted to show how great a respect he enjoyed among his fellow priests.

Among those present there were, beside the members of the City Council, the priest of the Chapel of St. Mary of the Court of the Binnenhof; the abbot of the Convent of St. Elisabeth, the monastery that occupied a large part of what today is the Great Market Square; the prior of St. Vincent's Monastery in the Voorhout, who was seated across from the mighty lords of Bethlehem Convent in the Assendelft Street and those of St. Agnes Convent that at that time was located in the Westeinde, approximately at the place now occupied by the Citizen's Orphanage. At the other end of the table were seated the chaplains of St. Mary's and Galilee Convents in the Lange Poten, and the chaplain of the Mary Chapel on the Spui or Spoon Bridge. Among the guests was even the old priest who served in the little chapel of "Our Lady with the Jars," which used to be situated at the Turnstile on the Scheveningen Road, the present-day Scheveningen Bridge. Indeed, the priest of St. Jacob's had spared neither pains nor expenses.

The most delicious sea fish, still living when they were brought over from Scheveningen that morning, was followed by the tastily prepared carp caught in the Hof pond. Immense pieces of beef and veal on large silver platters were succeeded by fried peacock, decorated with the colorful tail feathers, or by venison, as the woods near The Hague teemed with deer in those days.

Sweet Malvoisy wine sparkled in large goblets of Bohemian crystal alongside red wines that originated from southern France, which were poured as profusely as the golden wine that came from the banks of the Moselle and Rhine Rivers.

We have to mention that the guests did full justice to the royal meal; and not without reason history tells us that the Hollanders of those days were known as big eaters and still bigger drinkers.

One platter after another was emptied and the goblets, some of which contained almost two quarts, were emptied just as fast as they were filled by the servants hired for this occasion.

They drank to the health of Philip, king of Spain and lord of the Netherlands, and to that of the once mighty emperor, his father, who had retreated in a monastery; to the governess

An Important Dinner Conversation

and to the cardinal (Granvelle); to the prosperity of Holy Mother, the church, and to the extermination of all heretics.

Del Castro, who was always very controlled and serious, answered all these toasts with brief, beautiful phrases, and soon the moment arrived when stiff etiquette gave way to that happy, more excited atmosphere that derives its origin from the fermented juice of grapes.

But not every guest was excited or engaged in a lively conversation. At the lower end of the table, between the chaplain of St. Mary's Chapel and a huge brewer who was a member of the City Council, sat Cornelio, the Inquisitor's secretary, and he stared, somber and preoccupied, into space. He had hardly touched the richly ornamented platters and since his thoughts were elsewhere, he hardly took part in the conversations. He only touched his lips with his goblet when it was expected that he express his approval of a toast.

What could be the reason that Cornelio was so somber and reserved amid all this gaiety?

In Leyden, the farmer in "The Crown" had instilled a hope in him he had never entertained before. He had traveled with his master Del Castro to The Hague with the most beautiful plans, but alas, all his trouble had been in vain.

How his heart had started to beat faster when already from a great distance he had seen the tower of St. Jacob's Church! What tender and at the same time sad memories had flooded his soul when he, after a twelve-year absence, again trod the ground of his birth place! As a faithful son of the Roman Catholic Church, and as a child that honored the memory of his mother, his first trip had been to St. Jacob's Church in which his mother rested under a cold slab of granite.

It would be impossible for him ever to forget that place. Before he left The Hague, with his hand in his old cousin Anne-Bet's, he had visited his mother's grave and kneeling on the cold stone, had shed hot tears for her who had been taken away from him so early. It was then that he had greatly upset Anne-Bet when it became evident that his mother had not taught him to pray for the dead. Only later on his tutors had tried to explain that this was necessary for the soul's rest of his mother, and from that time on Cornelio had not let a month pass by without having at least one mass said for the eternal rest of his deceased mother.

Just as soon as his duties for the Inquisitor permitted it, he had gone out on an investigation in the Achterom, of which he had great expectations.

There he had seen the narrow, curving street again, which in rainy weather was one big mud pool, but which then had looked so pretty because of the snow and frost. Every house, even the awnings of the stores, had appeared to him as old acquaintances. The memories of his childhood days had flooded his soul and one after the other fought for his attention.

At last he had stood in front of the house in which he had been born and from which he had seen his mother being carried away. In his mind he had seen that the door was being opened and his father bending over him to embrace him before leaving to go on his trip. Nevertheless not everything looked the same as before. Later occupants had made various changes, and the fine room of his mother in the lower story had been made into a cloth shop.

Nothing would have been easier for Cornelio than to enter that shop and to inquire about the former occupants and if anything was known about them. But the secretary did not have enough courage to do so. Instead he looked left and right for the house of the shoemaker which the farmer in Leyden had so carefully described to him.

While Cornelio was looking around, a curious person appeared at his door, anxious to find out what he was looking for, but not being able to help him.

The shoemaker, whom Cornelio found after a while, had only recently moved into the Achterom and so was not able to give any information regarding the cheese merchant who had formerly lived in the house the secretary pointed out. The former shoemaker who had lived in the Achterom for many years had died long ago, and his wife had moved away; no one knew where.

And so Cornelio had searched and inquired, but not the least bit of evidence had turned up to confirm the information the farmer had given.

The Inquisitor's secretary was not yet sufficiently acquainted with conditions in Holland; otherwise he would have under-

An Important Dinner Conversation

stood why people were so little inclined to answer his questions. They were polite and uninhibited toward the priest of the parish to which they belonged, but they distrusted every other one, suspecting him to be a servant of the Inquisition, for even the most ardent Roman Catholics feared to appear before that religious court, whether as a suspect or as a witness.

Moreover, during the past twelve years the population in the center of the city had often changed and so Cornelio in his search had not succeeded in getting one step closer to his goal, and often asked himself whether the farmer in Leyden was mistaken.

After failing in his attempts, he had wondered whether he should ask for the help of Del Castro, but what could he really tell his master? That he had met a farmer in an inn, a man whose name he did not even know? What was the intelligent Inquisitor, who was so very experienced in every field, to think of his secretary? Certainly not much if the latter had not first ascertained himself of the trustworthiness and the name of his informant in a matter of such great importance.

So, during their stay in The Hague — which lasted much longer than Del Castro had expected, Cornelio had searched alone, hoping to learn something about his family, and had kept on hoping that fate would lead him to his father's tracks. And now the last day of their stay was almost past, and early the next morning the clerk would again leave The Hague with the Inquisitor. But would that farmer in Leyden have purposely deceived him?

All these things went through Cornelio's mind, and he heard neither the loud laughter of the fat brewer beside him nor the clanking of the glasses.

Del Castro, too, paid little attention to the clamor around him, as he was busily engaged in a conversation with the priest of St. Jacob's and the bailiff of The Hague.

Suddenly the clerk was disturbed in his reveries. It was the chaplain of St. Mary's Chapel on the Spoon Bridge who with a hard punch awoke him from his revery.

"What's the matter, friend, don't you like the wine, or in Louvain did they teach you not to drink? You know, when we were younger, we were not afraid of a few small casks, and even now I would dare to have a contest in drinking with your neighbor, the brewer!"

Laughing, the chaplain lifted his glass and viewed with the eye of a connoisseur the sparkling wine. His round cheeks, dark red in color from drinking so much wine, and his corpulent body, clearly indicated that the chaplain far more caressed than crucified his flesh, and that fasting certainly did not make him lose any weight.

"Come on," he continued, still speaking to Cornelio, "let's toast to the peace of these Lowlands and the extermination of the entire brood of heretics!"

At that moment neither one nor the other interested Cornelio in the least. Nevertheless he dutifully toasted with his neighbor to the left and to the right. "Not that way, but *ad fundum!* One would almost think that the secretary of the venerable Provincial Inquisitor wished the heretics good luck!"

"Even to suppose such a thing would be more than foolish," Cornelio answered, emptying his glass. "Nevertheless," he continued, "it is painful to see how from day to day this heresy spreads, and how the simple folk, misled by false teachers, become Satan's prey and suffer physical and spiritual loss."

"What you just said there certainly speaks well of your kind heart," the chaplain replied; "but as far as I am concerned, I quit feeling sorry for these people long ago, for most of them are rebels and firebrands of hell. But the worst part is that the more smarter and not conduct the executions publicly, because that does not seem to scare them off at all.

"In Amsterdam they understand this business far better. There they simply drown the stubborn heretics in a large wine vat filled with water, or they throw them, bound hand and foot, into the IJ River. Thus to be drowned like dogs robs these heretics of a martyr's glory!"

The chaplain of St. Mary's spoke about this manner of execution as if it were the most natural thing in the world. Cornelio, however, shuddered. He knew that the church, with the help of the civil authorities, took strong measures to halt the spread of heresy, but he did not know about this horrible way of disposing of these people who in all other respects were above reproach. "Does the church," he asked himself, "need to resort to such means to maintain itself?"

The more the chaplain drank, the more talkative he became. He went on, "It is particularly important to keep the youth away from heretical influences. In my limited circle I have seen the favorable result of doing just that. I still remember — it is years ago already — that one day a faithful parishioner of mine, an old woman who would have given and done anything for the church, asked me to come to the deathbed of a young woman in the Achterom."

Cornelio was startled when he heard the name of the street which had been on his mind all evening. But the chaplain, unconscious of this fact, continued, "It soon became apparent, however, that my help was neither desired nor in time. That woman — I believe she was Flemish — turned a deaf ear to all I said, and it proved to be not without reason that my parishioner had often told me in the confessional chair that she suspected her cousin of heretical tendencies, which she no doubt would teach her children as well.

"As was my duty, I tried to bring the dying woman to her senses and to show her her heresy that would certainly keep heaven's gate shut for her if she did not repent. But all was to no avail. Her only answer to all my questions was, 'I have peace through the blood of the cross!'

"You can imagine what kind of an upbringing this woman had given her child, a boy of about twelve at that time, be-they are being exterminated, the more their number increases. And what profit do they get from this new doctrine? Isn't the old teaching good enough? Hasn't it stood the test of time? And, besides, haven't we displayed in our churches the finest of all that art has to offer for the beautification of religion?

"True, my chapel does not contain much of that, but take St. Jacob's! Can you imagine anything more splendid and beautiful than the art treasures it contains? The main altar is renowned everywhere, and the choir is so richly adorned that one has to go all the way to Ghent and Bruges to find anything like it. Think of the statues and glorious altarpieces with the sunlight falling on them through stained-glass Gothic windows! And where else is the *Te Deum* sung as gloriously as in St. Jacob's? And yet these heretics prefer their sheds and caves where they sing their miserable songs they call psalms and with rapt attention listen to all that drivel that some tanner or fuller or traveling peddler, who can hardly read, preaches to them. These people must be crazy!"

"Yes, it is sad," Cornelio answered. "Still, I have asked myself at times whether we may not have emphasized the external too much to these people, and have not sufficiently satisfied the needs of their hearts. We indeed give the people all what we humanly can give them, but is that enough?"

"Ho, ho!" the corpulent chaplain interrupted him. "Is this the Inquisitor's secretary talking? One would almost think to be dealing with a heretic in disguise!"

"Don't take me up wrong," Cornelio answered; "far be it from me to defend this heresy. But this discontent with the situation as it always has been points it seems to me to a need, the satisfaction of which the heretics mistakenly seek elsewhere than in our holy church. I wish that our spiritual leaders would take measures to answer that need."

"See here, reverend, if you weren't the Inquisitor's clerk, I would really suspect you of entertaining heretical ideas. But in one respect I agree with you, namely, that correct steps should be taken. All these hangings and burnings and confiscations make matters worse rather than better. These things evoke the pity of the onlookers, and the destroyers of Holy Mother Church prey on that. The authorities should be

12

Mounting Doubts

For a long time Cornelio sat before the fireplace, his head resting in his hands. The chaplain's story had greatly shocked him and had thrown an entirely new light upon the life that lay behind him. Cornelio had no reason whatsoever to doubt whether people other than his parents might have been referred to in the chaplain's information. Even though the people in the Achterom had been either unable or unwilling to give him any information, the story he had heard from the chaplain of St. Mary's confirmed to a great extent that of the farmer in the inn at Leyden.

The more Cornelio thought about it the clearer it became to him that his education and his present position were the result of a single act — his removal from his parental home by his cousin Anne-Bet.

Until now he had always honored the memory of his old cousin as that of the woman who had taken him in, a poor orphan, and who had been the means, in spite of many difficulties and at great expense, that he had obtained an honorable position in the church. How entirely different her motives appeared to him now! By premeditated and sly manipulations he had been kidnapped from his parental home, and his whereabouts had been kept concealed from his father who, according to the chaplain's story, had escaped a terrible death

An Important Dinner Conversation 93

cause the father concerned himself little with that, as he was always traveling. So if I had left that boy in the care of his father, he certainly would have become a heretic too. Hence, upon my advice, the old woman took the lad with her and I showed her how to preserve his youthful soul for the church. When she visited me some time later on, the lad was being taken care of in a monastery school. Now I ask you, what would have become of that boy if I had not snatched him away from this evil environment?"

Cornelio did not answer that question. Instead he asked as nonchalantly as possible, "Did the father or the family assent to the boy's leaving home?"

"He had no other relatives than that old cousin whom I just mentioned. His father, it was first reported, had perished at sea a short time before that; but after a couple of weeks he turned up again. He even came to see me and inquired about his son, but as you realize yourself, the boy was in far better hands than those of a father who had tolerated a heretical wife. So I gave him no information, and after that I never heard anything about either him or his son anymore."

"And do you still remember the names of these people?" Cornelio asked.

"I don't remember their names anymore, but I believe that she was the wife of a cheese merchant who traveled in Flanders."

At that moment Del Castro arose, and all the guests followed his example. With a few well-chosen words he thanked his host, and bowed to the religious and civil dignitaries. Cornelio, too, bowed to the chaplain of St. Mary's and staggered out of the hall. Alone in his room he sat motionless for a long time, thinking about the story he had heard.

and had done everything he could to find his son. In his mind Cornelio went back to the time when he was still called Hidde and to the moment he had said farewell to his father for the last time. He could still picture the man who had kissed him, and even now after so many years, it was as if he saw the loving look in his father's eyes resting on him. And from this man, who must have grieved terribly when he did not find his wife after his return — from this father they had cruelly withheld the comfort of being able to press his elder son to his bosom.

"Is that showing interest in a poor orphan?" Cornelio asked bitterly, and involuntarily he doubled his fists.

How entirely different his youth would have been, he thought, if he had been allowed to stay with his father and little brother. In his mind Cornelio compared the loving treatment he had received from his parents with the harsh treatment in the monastery school. Until now he had always considered that school as an inevitable necessity; now it appeared to him as an unnecessary cruelty. Anne-Bet and the chaplain had robbed him of the love of his father, the affection of a brother, and an environment in which he had been happy.

Contrary to their better knowledge, they had told him that his little brother was dead and they had never told him that his father had searched for him. Cornelio asked himself how such base conduct could coincide with the dignity of the priesthood. Could anything more wicked be imagined? One thing he marveled about now was that he had been able to control himself so well when the chaplain had told him about his kidnapping. Angrily he arose and walked up and down the room. "Tomorrow," he said out loud, "tomorrow I am going to look him up and show him the result of what he has done! And I am going to heap upon his head all the bitterness that all these years has accumulated in my heart. And I won't let go of him until he has told me where I can find my father and brother, for he must know where they are."

Just then a servant entered his room with the message that the Inquisitor wished to see him and was waiting for him.

Cornelio was not in the mood, however, to present himself to Del Castro, and he told the servant to tell his master that after the party he had been plagued with a splitting headache and was hardly able to move himself. Again he sat down in the easy chair in front of the fireplace.

"Was there any good reason that justified the action of the old chaplain?" he asked himself. They had wanted to take him away from heretical influences; that was obvious, and from that point of view Cornelio had to agree with the chaplain, albeit reluctantly. But what proved that in his youth he had lived in a heretical environment?

He had never heard that his father had embraced the new doctrine; and even the chaplain of St. Mary's had not claimed that. The only thing was that his father had tolerated a heretical wife. Cornelio shuddered at the thought that his mother might have been a heretic. But still, what the chaplain had told him was bad enough. On her deathbed she had refused the means of grace of Holy Mother Church! Refused!

Could it be true? Cornelio could not imagine that. Only hardened, wicked heretics could commit such a mortal sin. Yet it was of this sin that the chaplain had accused his mother. But even if she had committed such a lamentable error, there was no doubt that this was due to her illness; but then, too, she could not be held accountable for such a sin!

Still, what was the meaning of her constant calling, "I have peace through the blood of the cross?" Those were her last words, according to the chaplain of St. Mary's. Peace through the blood of the cross — could a heretic ever have peace? Could a heretic ever enter eternity with peace in his heart? Would that not be a false peace, invented by Satan, that great enemy of souls, to blindfold the faithful sons and daughters of the church in order to cast them into eternal perdition? Indeed, at the University of Louvain Cornelio had often heard of heretics who had supposedly even prayed at the stake. Those stories had been told in whispers and had passed from one to the other because the authorities watched with the utmost care — and severity — that nothing was said that placed the heretics in a favorable light.

Was it possible that there was peace outside Mother Church — a peace which Cornelio did not know? For was not peace with God the only true peace? And if such a peace were based on the blood of the cross, how could it be a false peace? "But

Mounting Doubts

of such a peace the Church does not know," Cornelio thought. All she could give was hope, but never certainty, to those who were obedient to her. Was, then, the peace of which his mother had boasted when she cast her dying eyes to heaven greater than the peace the Church offered?

The longer Cornelio thought about these things the more his thoughts multiplied; and although he did not yet want to admit it, doubt arose in his soul. The question forced itself upon him, "Do I myself have peace — the peace of which St. Paul speaks and which surpasses all understanding?"

Suddenly Cornelio startled. He had been so immersed in thought that he had not noticed that the Provincial Inquisitor had quietly entered the room, and not until the latter put his hand on Cornelio's shoulder did he wake up as from a dream.

"Cornelio," Del Castro started, slowly and seriously, "you are hiding something from me. No, no! you may not deny it," he continued reprimandingly when the clerk made a slight motion as in denial. "For a couple of days already I have carefully watched you, and even tonight not a word or movement on your part has escaped my attention in spite of all the commotion at dinner.

"I can understand that seeing again the place where you spent the first years of your life would rather affect you; but you may not allow it to go so far as to make you lose sight of your calling! And so I ask you in all seriousness, not as your father confessor but as one who is greatly concerned about your welfare: What is the reason for your isolating yourself and for being so quiet when others are happy? There must be a reason for your being so depressed; and although I have an idea what it is, I nevertheless would like to hear it from your own lips. The mood you are in is wholly foreign to your age. Come," he continued, taking Cornelio's hand in his, "tell me the secrets of your heart. You know, I am not without influence and maybe I can solve your problems."

The Inquisitor spoke these last words in a fatherly, almost tender, tone of voice, wholly suitable to win Cornelio's heart which was very receptive to a kind word.

Rancor and anger gave way to a feeling of deep sorrow, and tears welled from the eyes of the young priest. Del Castro pulled a chair over and sat down beside Cornelio.

"Come, my son, unburden your heart and tell me what is bothering you."

Cornelio was not able to resist such prompting. With a trembling voice that betrayed both grief and anger he told of his vain attempts to find some trace of his relatives in the Achterom and of what he had heard afterwards from the chaplain at dinner.

"The last part I already know," Del Castro answered. "After you left the hall I asked the old and in every respect venerable priest of St. Mary's to tell me what he had said to you, since I had concluded from the few words which I had been able to catch at dinner that his story seemed to be important to you. But what made you go and search in the Achterom in the first place? For at that time you had not talked with the chaplain yet."

Cornelio's face turned red. To his embarrassment he now had to tell what the farmer in "The Crown" at Leyden had told him; to his embarrassment, because he had kept this secret for such a long time from Del Castro.

The Inquisitor thought for a while. "This certainly is a remarkable incident," he began, "and I can fully understand that all you have heard during the last days could lead you astray and cause you to draw false conclusions. I even believe that if you had let your mind be your guide instead of your heart, you would soon have come to entirely different conclusions. From the manner in which you have told me your story it is quite obvious that you take the man referred to by that unknown farmer and the cheese merchant mentioned by the chaplain of St. Mary's to be one and the same person. As far as I am concerned nothing substantiates that conclusion. There is absolutely nothing to prove the fact that your father did not perish and therefore it rests only on a rumor. The story the chaplain told is no doubt true, but when you consider his age, and the changing populace of a city such as The Hague, how can you so quickly jump to conclusions and take two different persons to be one and the same man? Do you really believe that if your father were still alive you would never have heard from him all these years? Do you really think that he would have given up after the first unsuccessful attempt to find you and accepted the fact that you were lost?"

"I would never believe that!" Cornelio interrupted the Inquisitor. "But they kept him in the dark about my whereabouts!"

Del Castro bit his thin lip. "They! — who are 'they,' Cornelio?"

Cornelio could not answer that question.

"They," Del Castro continued in the same good-natured tone of voice as a moment before, "had not the least personal interest in mind when they educated you for a position in the Church. If the person referred to in the chaplain's story was indeed you, 'they' would certainly have found many other ways to keep you from the pestilence of heresy. But suppose that the cheese merchant was indeed your father, then you must also admit that the woman at whose deathbed he stood was your mother. In that case, can you imagine anything more horrible than such a deathbed — dying, and refusing the hand of the priest who offers the means of grace of the Church; dying, and denying Christ's injunction to His servants, 'Whatsoever ye shall bind on earth shall be bound in heaven: and whatsoever ye shall loose on earth shall be loosed in heaven'? If that woman was indeed your mother — which I don't believe — then you should consider yourself fortunate indeed that you are in a position, and have so many means at your disposal, to make up for so much mishap. By wholly consecrating yourself to the service of the Church you can restore all that which through no fault of yours has been ruined. Now look," Del Castro continued, seeing that his words were not without impact on Cornelio, "a wide field of labor lies open before you. The realm which Emperor Charles has made great is threatened with destruction. A false doctrine invented by Satan's instrument, Martin Luther, is daily destroying the souls of the faithful. Weavers and fullers, coopers and all kinds of unlearned folk imagine in their arrogance that they can show the multitudes the way to heaven, even though these so-called leaders hardly know how to read. I feel sorry for these misled multitudes, for these simple, erring souls. And I will treat them with softness and moderation. But these deceivers of the people, these open-air preachers, these murderers of souls, these enemies of our Holy Church will feel all my fury. I shall exterminate their entire number, which daily grows on account of the gentleness of the governess! And in this task,

Cornelio, you will have a part. It is a task that will be crowned with a heavenly crown because it is pleasing to God. Remember the solemn oath you took at your consecration! Ours is the battle cry of the Israelites when they fought the Philistines. We know only one command: Exterminate all who wish to destroy the ancient heritage of the Church! In this battle we cannot be concerned about father or mother, brother or sister! Especially for you the words of Scripture are relevant: 'He that loveth father or mother more than me is not worthy of me!'"

Del Castro said these last words standing up and with his left hand raised, while his right hand held Cornelio's.

"What do you think, Cornelio," he asked; "isn't that a beautiful calling? And would you hesitate to join our ranks if you were considered worthy to do your part in such a noble, such a holy cause?"

Cornelio did not answer. The words which the Inquisitor had spoken with such fervor and enthusiasm stirred only the surface of his soul, but they did not penetrate to its depth, for there doubts had awakened and these Del Castro had neither suspected nor removed.

"Tomorrow," Del Castro went on, "we are going to Amsterdam. I have received word that one of the most dangerous open-air preachers has fallen into our hands and I am going to let you take part in the prosecution of this heretic, to show you how much I trust you."

13

At Duivenvoorde Castle

After the people at Hannes's house had somewhat gotten over their fright from the sudden appearance of the king's servants and the apprehension of Harm Hiddesz, they looked at each other, wondering what to do in this difficult situation.

There they sat — Hannes, his wife, and Melis — in the large room where a few days before the friends from the neighborhood had gathered; and they had to admit to each other that their situation was precarious indeed. Up in the alcove lay the small dead body of the boy on whose pale, stiff face there still was an expression of heavenly joy. What were they to do with him? The Fleming's threat that he would soon return could be carried out at any time. They did not conceal from each other that they were subject to severe punishment because they had lodged a heretic, and though they knew that the Inquisition sought him, they had hidden him. For the first time they fully realized the danger to which they had exposed themselves. As long as Harm Hiddesz had been in their midst, they had thought of nothing else but his safety and a way of escape for him; but now matters were wholly different. Now they had to think of their own safety. Who could help them, however? There was only One into whose care they could entrust themselves, the only One who could help His oppressed people when human help failed.

"We shall take it to the Lord," Hannes said in his simpleness; "the God who alone doeth wonders can give us light in our darkness and show us what we must do."

"But where is Bouke?" the woman asked. "He must pray with us."

Indeed, where was Bouke? Melis had seen how he had followed the soldiers when they took off with Harm, but it was unthinkable that Bouke would have gone away without first telling them where he was going. Hannes and Melis called his name in the stable and around the yard, but they got no answer. Now the farmer's wife became very concerned, and Melis was sent to the ferryhouse to inquire whether Bouke had been there.

After a short while Melis returned, out of breath from running so fast, and with an expression of alarm on his face.

"Quick, Hannes!" he said to his brother-in-law, "come along with me; I am afraid that Bouke has met with an accident!"

"What happened!" cried the woman, wringing her hands in apprehension.

"I don't know," Melis replied, "but we'll be back soon!"

The two men sped away with the sleigh which Melis had taken out of the barn in no time at all.

"Oh Lord," sighed the woman, "Thou knowest what will happen to us next."

Before half an hour had passed, the two men returned and carefully carried the body of the farmhand inside.

Mrs. Hannes nearly fainted when she saw the blood-covered face of the faithful servant and friend of her youth.

"He's dead!" she wailed.

"No, it isn't as bad as that," Melis said, "but I believe that it would not have taken much longer, because it is bitter cold outside. Just feel," he said to Hannes, "his heart is still beating. But how come he is all covered with blood?"

After a careful examination they discovered quite a large wound at the back of Bouke's head. The cold and the snow had prevented his bleeding to death. In the warm room Bouke soon regained consciousness, and after they had washed and bandaged him, he was able to tell them what had happened to him.

At Duivenvoorde Castle

In spite of their gratitude that Bouke had not become the victim of his rashness, they realized, however, that their situation was now even more precarious than before. The interference by their farmhand would be charged against them as well, and would certainly not go unpunished.

The longer they discussed the situation the greater their need became to ask light and wisdom from on high, and if "miserly Aart" would have looked through the slits of the shutters a few minutes afterwards, he would have seen the foursome on their knees, and would have heard Hannes's fervent entreaty to God to remember His promise never to leave nor forsake His poor and oppressed people in their distress.

Strengthened by their united prayer, they again discussed the matter, and soon agreed that it was advisable to call in the help of the lord of Duivenvoorde, for he liked Hannes's family and with him the farmer's wife would always find an attentive ear. Once they had arrived at this decision, it seemed to them that the greatest danger had passed, and they prepared to go to bed. But first they all went to the little room where Adriaan lay.

"Have you cut off a lock of his hair?" asked Bouke, who remembered the lad's last words.

"What would be the use, now that his father is gone?" asked Mrs. Hannes.

Bouke, who never spoke much, shrugged his shoulders and, after having left the room for a few minutes, returned with a pair of scissors and clipped off one of the long, blond locks of hair, which he carefully wrapped in a piece of paper and put away.

Solemnly and with tears in her eyes the woman pulled the sheet over the boy.

"Look," Hannes said, reaching for the little Bible at the foot of the bed, "how the poor man must miss that precious book which for so many years accompanied him, now that he has to go through such a deep valley!"

Bouke picked up the little book.

"What do you want to do with it?" Hannes asked.

"I am going to take it, with the lock of hair of his child, to Master Harm!" was the reply.

They all looked at him in astonishment.

"How? When?" they all asked at the same time.

"I don't know yet, but you all heard that Master Harm has received a promise that he would find his older son, and this child, who is now in heaven singing praises to God, has confirmed that, and he has said that a lock of his hair must be given to his brother. How can the master carry this out if he does not have such a lock of hair?" asked Bouke.

"But, Bouke, you know that Harm Hiddesz has been carried off to prison!" the woman replied.

"Certainly I know that!" Bouke said, putting his hand to his head where the wound, painfully enough, reminded him of the sad fact.

The next morning, just when the farmer's wife got ready to go to the castle of the lord of Duivenvoorde, a strange man from Leyden knocked at the door and asked if Hannes lived there. Upon her affirmative answer the man handed her a note written by Harm Hiddesz. It was the first word from the prisoner, but it contained nothing more than a request to give his mantle along with the carrier of the note. The woman immediately got the mantle and asked the man how the prisoner was and where he was.

"The man is at present in the Stone," was the reply, "and is waiting there, together with a few others of his kind, for an opportunity to be taken to Amsterdam."

"To Amsterdam?" asked the woman in surprise. "And why not to The Hague? Isn't that where the Court is and where all court matters of this area must be adjudged?"

Now it was the messenger's turn to look puzzled.

"I don't know about those things, woman," he answered. "Those are things I don't concern myself with, and I think it is advisable that you don't either. The members of the Court have long arms, and if I were you, I wouldn't meddle in these things, because if I am not mistaken you are fonder of the heretic than is good for you."

He took the mantle and mumbling a greeting, left.

With a burdened heart and full of concern about the outcome, the woman, accompanied by Hannes, went on her way.

At Duivenvoorde Castle

The couple had quite a trip ahead of them. After they had crossed the Vliet over the ice, near the ferryhouse, they followed a narrow lane bordered by alder trees that led to Voorschoten. Passing through the village it appeared to them that many people who always used to greet them kindly now turned their heads and pointed a finger at them after they had passed them. The news that the heretic, after having hid himself for several days at their house and had been apprehended, had preceded Hannes and his wife. They still had to travel more than half an hour over the frozen ground covered with snow before they reached the old castle so familiar to them. The closer they got to the house of their landlord, however, the more perturbed they became. For a minute the woman thought that it might be best to tell the lord of Duivenvoorde everything that had taken place, but Hannes rejected the idea. He was of the opinion that in this case, too, it was best to combine the harmlessness of doves with the wisdom of serpents.

When they arrived at the castle, Hannes stayed behind, since they had agreed that it was best that his wife would see the lord alone.

With pounding heart and not without many silent prayers she waited in the large front hall for the return of the servant who had gone to the lord of Duivenvoorde to inform him of her arrival. As expected, she was immediately admitted and soon the farmer's wife was standing in the large, medieval room before the landlord.

The lord of Duivenvoorde was sitting in a large chair before the fireplace; his left leg was resting on a wooden footstool as he was sorely afflicted with gout, especially during the winter months. When this painful disease attacked him, the old nobleman was very irritable, and often curt and unreasonable to his subjects.

"Well, Brechtje," the landlord said in a rather friendly tone of voice, "what brought you here? I hope no accident took place on the farm? As you see," he continued, "I am being bothered by my old trouble again, but today my old enemy is rather quiet. Sit down a while and tell me what's on your mind. But before you start with your own story, tell me first what are those strange rumors that have reached my ears? So many contradictory things have been told me that I am truly happy to see you in person."

Brechtje, as Hannes's wife was always called at the castle, modestly sat down on the chair the lord of Duivenvoorde had pointed out to her.

"It is precisely about the things that have taken place at my house," she said, "that I have come to talk to you and to ask your advice, lord. We are but simple folk, as your lordship knows, and when we are in difficulty, we simply come here because my lord is always ready to assist us with word and deed.

"Certainly, certainly!" the landlord said, flattered by the introduction to Brechtje's story, "You have acted very wisely by doing so."

Brechtje continued, "My brother-in-law, Melis — my lord no doubt remembers him — on the day before Christmas met a traveler or peddler at the ferryhouse who had a young boy with him who was deathly sick. And since the lad could go no farther — these people had to go to Leyden — and there was no room at the ferryhouse for them to stay, he took the man and the sick child in a sleigh to our house."

"Melis always was a faithful fellow," the nobleman interrupted her.

"If only the lad had recovered, the man would at once have continued on his way the next day, which we would have liked much better. But the boy got sicker and sicker, and the poor child lay in his bed groaning with a fever. Would I have done right if I had sent that man and his child away, and should I have allowed myself to be the cause of that child's dying outside in the bitter cold?"

"Absolutely not! That you did not learn when you served here. The virtue of hospitality has never been neglected here!"

"Nevertheless, what I have done has been taken very evil. Strange soldiers broke into our house and took the man prisoner, claiming that he was a heretic!"

"What?" interrupted the lord of Duivenvoorde, "who dares to meddle in things that concern only me? Am I not the lord of the Manor of Voorschoten and Dependency? Do not I alone have the authority to deal with legal matters, both high and low?" Angrily the old nobleman thumped the floor with his cane which stood beside his chair. "Who were these usurpers?"

"I don't know, noble lord! They came in the name of the king."

"Only I act here in the name of the king! But go on."

"One of the soldiers demanded wine, and I gave him the only jar I had in the house, the crock that my lord sent for my husband a while back."

The nobleman clenched his fist.

"After they had been drinking for a long time they finally wanted to take the prisoner away, but he had escaped and they had to leave without him."

"I am happy to hear that!" the landlord interrupted the woman; "I love to see that poachers in my territory miss the game and have to go home with empty bags!"

"After the soldiers had left, it appeared that the man had hid himself in our house. So what were we to do? We could not chase him away in the night and put his almost-dying child in the snow on the dike, could we?"

"Of course not!" the old man wholeheartedly agreed.

"So he stayed for a few days longer with us, hoping that his young son would get well again. Alas! That was not to be. Yesterday the dear child died; it almost seemed as if he were my own child; that's how attached I already had become to the lad." Saying this, the woman began to cry.

"After the strange merchant had pressed the eyes of his child shut," she continued, "suddenly the same strange soldiers appeared again, and they bound the man and took him with them. And so I have come to your lordship for advice. What must we do? The dead body of that strange child lies in our house. The priest of Voorschoten will no doubt refuse to bury him, and who knows into how much trouble we will get yet because they caught this man in our house. They have already threatened to drag us out of our home because we have, so they say, been in league with heretics. Is that to be the reward for our hospitality, and is Melis to be dragged to the Stone like a scoundrel simply because he has a sympathetic heart? Am I, who have served your lordship so faithfully for so many years, to languish in prison with my husband? Is the lord of Duivenvoorde going to tolerate that this shame shall descend upon us and our home for no other reason than that we have done a duty which I learned to observe here in your house?"

"None of these things will happen; of that you can be sure!" angrily cried the lord of Duivenvoorde, "but I know where the shoe pinches here. The priests are behind all this. They should have informed and consulted me, and if any offenses have to be punished I shall show them that I know the placards of the emperor and the king as well as all the best of all priests together. And now, Brechtje, you just go home. I shall immediately instruct my steward to see to it that the boy gets a decent burial. And if the priest of Voorschoten dares to object, I shall show him who is master and lord here. This very day I am going to write a letter to the Court of Holland, and I am demanding custody of the man who was apprehended in your house. The claim has been made that an offense has been committed in my territory. Well, I am going to investigate that, and no one else! So, don't worry. I shall make it clear to the gentlemen in The Hague and anywhere else that they must keep their hands off my territory and my people!"

Brechtje, now wholly put at ease, left; and Hannes, who had not felt the cold east wind on account of his great fear, could already tell by the happy expression on her face that she had not been disappointed.

After Hannes and Melis had heard Brechtje's story, they all thanked God for His mercy, because it is He who governs the hearts of the high and the mighty and inclines His ear to the supplications of His children.

14

In "The Stone" at Leyden

Willingly Harm Hiddesz had let himself be carried off by the Flemish captain. Resistance would have been futile anyway.

When they got to the ferryhouse, he looked for the last time back to the place where he had left behind the mortal remains of his dear child in Hannes's house. Sighing silently, although inwardly comforted, he followed, with increased speed and in between two halberdiers, the Fleming and Antonio, who had mounted their horses again at the ferryhouse. On the way Harm heard the story of the fight with Bouke, and with horror he learned that Antonio had struck the servant down and had left him for dead. His heart bled at the thought that Bouke's faithfulness to and love of a persecuted preacher had driven him to resistance and that he had become the victim of his readiness to help.

Harm Hiddesz did not have much time for contemplation however. He was constantly urged to greater speed as the Fleming wanted to get to Leyden before the closing of the city gates. In this he scarcely succeeded because the watchmen at the North Gate were just preparing to shut the doors and raise the heavy bridge when the group entered the city where the Inquisitor had stayed only a few days before.

The men went immediately to "The Stone," the gloomy, square building near St. Peter's Church, into which Harm Hiddesz, shivering from the cold, was taken.

After the captain had showed his papers to the jailer, the latter took the prisoner into custody and Harm was led away through a dark corridor. Then a heavy door with many bolts and locks was opened and in the light of the lantern which the jailer's servant carried in his hand Harm Hiddesz could see a rather large room in which a few people were huddled together on a heap of straw.

"Must I stay here for the night?" Harm Hiddesz asked.

"Certainly," was the reply, "this temporary cell is no palace, to be sure, but who could expect that! At any rate, it is good enough for heretics like you."

Harm Hiddesz entered the room. It was chilly and damp because, although there was a fireplace, there was no fire in it.

"I presume that for payment one can get some wood and a couple of candles?" Harm asked.

"Certainly," the man answered, "for as long as you are locked up in this room you can get anything you want as long as you have money to pay for it."

Harm put his hand into his jerkin and gave the jailer a coin. "I should also very much like to have a warm drink and some bread," he said. Then the jailer and his servant departed, leaving him behind in the darkness.

For a moment it was quiet. Nothing but the footsteps of the men in the dark corridors could be heard.

"Am I deceiving myself?" suddenly a voice said in a corner of the room. "I believe I recognize the voice of the man who was expected to be here at Christmas!" It seemed that the person who said this purposely avoided mentioning names.

"You may freely call me by my name, my friend," was Harm's reply. "But wait just a few minutes. When I get a light I shall no doubt recognize you, and although your voice does not sound strange to me, I must nevertheless make sure that I am not dealing with a spy."

Sooner than Harm Hiddesz had expected the servant returned, and after a while the light of a candle and the flames of some faggots gave an entirely different perspective to the gloomy room.

A few moments later the servant returned once more with a large kettle of hot barley water and placed a loaf of bread on the only wooden bench in the entire room. Harm asked the servant to have someone sent for his mantel at Hannes's house, which the man gladly consented to do himself in return for a sizable payment, allowing the prisoner to write a few words on a slip of paper.

After the servant had left, there was some stirring in the corner and a man walked over to Harm, calling him by his name.

Amazement and joy expressed themselves on the face of the preacher. He recognized Folkert, the vegetable grower, at whose house near the Gallows Gate he had been expected on Christmas Day. The two men greeted each other with the utmost warmth and joy. This meeting on the pathway of persecution and suffering was a great comfort to them.

"Why, friend, must I meet you here?" Harm said to Folkert. "And have you been here a long time?"

"Since the day before Christmas, dear friend. But I am not an object of pity, even though I have suffered much from the cold and discomfort here, as I did not have the money to buy anything from the jailer beside what he is supposed to give us. On the contrary, I have spent here hours of heavenly communion with my Redeemer and Savior. In the darkness He was my Light, the Star of Judah, upon whom my eyes were allowed to gaze. When I spent the Christmas days here in solitude, I meditated on the incarnation of the only-begotten Son who according to the counsel of the Father bore the sin and guilt of His elect people and obtained eternal salvation for them. I rejoiced in God, and the Lord enabled me to sing psalms in the night. And now that He has deemed me worthy to witness to the faith which His Spirit had wrought in my heart, I am, in spite of my bondage, freer than a bird and richer than a king!"

"Why, friend," Harm said, "if that is how matters are with you, then I rejoice with you. This truly is a confirmation of what Paul says, 'We glory in tribulations also; knowing that tribulation worketh patience, and patience, experience; and experience, hope: and hope maketh not ashamed; because the love of God is shed abroad in our hearts by the Holy Ghost which is given unto us.'"

"That I have experienced," Folkert said, "for with David I could say, 'He restoreth my soul: He leadeth me in the paths of righteousness for His Name's sake. Yea, though I walk through the valley of the shadow of death, I will fear no evil: for Thou art with me; Thy rod and Thy staff they comfort me.' Even this noon, when we broke our meager piece of bread and had nothing to drink but cold water from a jar, I could say with gladness in my heart, 'Lord, Thou preparest a table before me in the presence of mine enemies: Thou anointest my head with oil; my cup runneth over'! And now the Lord brings you here and prepares through your hand our table."

Folkert looked rather longingly at the kettle that was steaming on the fire and at the large loaf of whole wheat bread which the jailer's servant had brought in. Although the spiritual man in Folkert sang praises, it was obvious that his body had suffered want for several days. In a brotherly manner, Harm shared the simple food which to Folkert seemed like a festive meal. As soon as Harm had broken the bread and filled Folkert's stone cup, the latter walked over to the corner of the room which Harm had not yet noticed.

"Come on, mother," Folkert said, "take a warm drink. It will do you good!"

Astonished, Harm went over to the group. On the straw two women were huddled together and both eagerly reached for the warm barley water and shared the contents of the cup together.

"This woman," Folkert said, pointing at the younger of the two, "is a poor widow who frequently attended our meetings. She is now separated from her children after her neighbors betrayed her. And the other one," Folkert continued, pointing at the older woman, "is her sister. She is a 'relapse.'" (A "relapse" was a person who during trial renounced his or her belief. Usually such a person was condemned to death by the inquisitors when he or she fell into their hands a second time.) "But she is determined, with God's grace, not to deny the Lord and His cause again. Isn't that right, Mrs. Baltens?"

"Ah, my dear friend Folkert, how I have regretted that I, like Peter, in the hour of danger have valued the safety of my body higher than the honor of Christ. It is my fervent desire that He will give me, miserable wretch, the necessary strength so that I do not succumb a second time."

"And you, mother," Harm asked, "do you feel strong enough to face the coming trial? Don't you dread the prospect of possibly having to lay down your life for the name of the Lord?"

"At times," replied the woman, "my flesh trembles at the thought of a martyr's death at the hands of the cruel wicked, but when grace reigns in my heart, I can be not only reconciled with, but also rejoice in, the fact that I shall be offered as a drink offering to the Lord Jesus. Nevertheless, there are times that I am bowed down under one great burden which I hope the Lord in His time will take away from me entirely. I am a poor widow. My older son is a boy of twelve and I have also a younger one who is just three years old. These poor lambs are now with strangers. During the night it is as if I hear little Leendert call for his mother! And that makes me scared and oppresses me until I commit my burdens to the Lord again for a time. May He increase my faith and loosen me from everything that is outside of Him!"

When she said this, the woman began to cry and lifted her folded hands up to heaven.

"Poor mother," Harm Hiddesz sighed. "The Lord leads you through deep ways. But cling to Him; lean and rest upon His unchangeable faithfulness. He will not forsake you, nor leave you. I too am greatly afflicted. This very afternoon I saw my only child, also a boy twelve years old, depart, but I may believe that my Adriaan now sings God's praises before the throne of the Lamb."

It seemed that Harm's last words had touched the most tender snares of the woman's heart because she now started to weep out loud.

"Let the woman weep," Harm said. "I shall tell her how my Adriaan passed away. And I shall remind her, in the name of the Lord and to her comfort, of God's promise by the mouth of Isaiah: 'As for me, this is my covenant with them, saith the Lord: My spirit that is upon thee, and My words which I have put in thy mouth, shall not depart out of thy mouth, nor out of the mouth of thy seed, nor out of the mouth of thy seed's seed, saith the Lord, from henceforth and forever.'"

In "The Stone" at Leyden 115

Then Harm Hiddesz recounted everything that had happened during the last few days while he stayed at Hannes's — his initial miraculous escape, the death of his child, and his recapture. And if the flickering of the dying candlelight had not reminded them that it was getting late, they would have kept talking and telling each other their experiences.

So the two men and two women knelt together; and the Lord Jesus who said, "Where two or three are gathered together in My Name, there I am in the midst of them," was at that late hour also present in the cell of "The Stone."

Harm Hiddesz had spent only two days there — days of mutual comforting and encouraging each other — when the Fleming returned from his trip to The Hague. From the Inquisitor he brought orders with him to have Harm Hiddesz, the "relapse," and her sister removed to Amsterdam.

The lord of Duivenvoorde, determined as he was, had immediately after Brechtje's visit sent a messenger to The Hague to claim the prisoner Harm Hiddesz, something which, on account of the existing judicial customs of those days, could hardly be refused.

Del Castro had learned of the nobleman's action at the Court of the Hague, and now made haste to get his prey to a safe place. So Harm Hiddesz had to be removed with the utmost speed to Amsterdam, outside of the jurisdiction of the Court of Holland; and the Fleming had been charged to get a wagon to transport the preacher and the two women under sufficient supervision.

We shall not describe the farewell scene when all three said goodbye to Folkert. The pious gardener embraced all three as if they were his brother and sisters whom he would not see again on this earth.

It grieved him that he was not included in the Fleming's orders; but Harm, who had a word of comfort for each of them, told him that the Lord certainly must have other plans for him, that He no doubt had some work for him to do, and that therefore he did not have to appear before the Court as yet.

To make Folkert's prolonged stay at "The Stone" — be it for a shorter or longer period of time — somewhat bearable,

Harm gave him a few coins which would have more influence on the jailer than the softest words.

In a crude, linen-covered wagon, accompanied by two armed horsemen, Harm Hiddesz and the two women began their journey to Amsterdam.

It was a bad journey for the three friends. The heavy frost, which had been so severe for a long time, had given way to cold, rainy weather. No kind sunshine fell on field or roadway; on the contrary, it seemed as if nature, too, did its part to fill the three travelers with gloom. After the hours of rejoicing they had spent in "The Stone" they were now filled with a sadness and fear of all the terrors that lay ahead of them so that their souls were cast down and disquieted within them. Master Harm greatly missed his Bible, the faithful companion that so often had encouraged him and others in days of affliction. But the Holy Spirit came to the aid of his memory, and from time to time he repeated the words of the Psalms of David to himself and the women, the psalms which had been composed by the man after God's heart in days of adversity.

Mrs. Balten's sister was constantly being assailed by Satan. That old murderer of men kept on trying to keep this weak soul from seeking refuge in Christ and to cast her into darkness and despair.

"Just what have you gained," he whispered to her, "by following this new teaching? What else but contempt, suffering, and an untimely death will it bring you! How can a mother, for the sake of a novelty, entrust her children to strangers? And why did you have to expose your so-called faith? What will now become of those children? When they have become grown-ups they will curse their unloving mother! And do you think that you are strong enough to endure the tortures of the rack during your examination? Ah, when they but apply the thumbscrews, your faith will fly away like chaff before the wind!"

Satan's darts were sharp and wounded the poor woman's flesh; but they did not succeed in killing the life of God within her soul. And both women repeated the words of Psalm 42 which Harm Hiddesz had recited a moment ago: "As with a sword in my bones, mine enemies reproach me: while they say daily unto me, Where is thy God? Why art thou cast down, O my soul? and why art thou disquieted within me? Hope thou in God: for I shall yet praise Him, who is the health of my countenance, and my God."

After six hours of riding on the jerking, bumping wagon, they saw the towers of Amsterdam in the distance.

"Do you have any idea, master Harm, where we are being taken?" Mrs. Baltens asked.

"No, I don't," Harm answered. "They will possibly lock us up in St. Olaf's Gate, because that usually serves as a prison. In Amsterdam they also use as prisons St. Anthony's Gate, the Tower of Our Lady, John Roden's Gate and Holy Cross Tower. I quite know my way around in Amsterdam and I also have a few friends here. I hope at least that they have managed to stay out of the hands of the Inquisition, because I have not heard from them for quite some time. Heretics are also taken to the Herring Packers' Tower, although women are often imprisoned in convents."

The women sighed.

"Ah," Mrs. Baltens said, "if only the Lord will make us faithful, then it makes no difference where they take us. No matter how much they will torment us, I know this, that nothing shall separate us from the love of Christ; and, sister," said the woman who felt the courage of her faith grow stronger again, "is it not a great comfort that in this our flesh we shall see God?"

"'Whom I shall see for myself, and mine eyes shall behold, and not another,'" Harm Hiddesz continued, and lifting up his eyes to heaven, he exulted with Job: "My reins are consumed with longing within me!"

The wagon entered the fortified city of Amsterdam and soon stopped before Holy Cross Tower. When Harm Hiddesz noticed that they stopped in front of this place, which already at that time was notorious, he looked with great concern at the two women. It would have been very appropriate if above its entrance the words had been chiseled which Dante, the Italian poet, in imagination had read above the entrance to hell: "Let all who enter here, abandon all hope!"

Was not this tower a place of weeping and wailing so that part of the N. Z. Achterburgwal was called Martyrs' Canal and to which Blood Street owes its name?

The horsemen told the three friends to get down from the wagon and led them through the front gate, where a couple of soldiers were sitting inside near the hearth playing cards.

The jailer took the sealed letter from one of the soldiers and scanned its contents. "Mr. Del Castro seems to be in a hurry," he muttered. "But that's just as well, for if things continue the way they are, there will soon be no room anymore." He then wrote a few words on a piece of paper, and with a string attached a seal to it and gave it to the horseman as proof that the latter had turned over the prisoners in good order.

Without speaking one word to the prisoners he gave a few commands to the servants who at the ringing of a bell had entered the room and led the three friends away.

"Do we stay together?" Harm asked one of the servants when they entered the corridor.

"Oh, no! That would be against the rules that forbid locking up men and women in the same room except in cases of emergency. For the time being the women will be kept upstairs, but we have to take you down below."

When they reached the winding stone stairs where the three friends had to be separated, Harm was overcome with emotion. He knew only too well what all this indicated. He shook hands with the two women. "The Lord be your Strength! May He be your Refuge! Farewell! We shall meet one another again before the throne of the Lamb!" was all Harm Hiddesz could utter.

Mrs. Baltens, the "relapse," was in high spirits, however. It seemed as though the gloom of the place where she had been taken had cheered instead of depressed her.

"Keep courage, dear friend," said the weak woman to the strong man, the faithful preacher who had survived so many trying ordeals in the past. "'The Spirit itself beareth witness with our spirit, that we are the children of God: and if children, then heirs: heirs of God, and joint-heirs with Christ: if so be that we suffer with Him that we may be also glorified together.'"

The jailer's servants urged the women to cut it short. The friends shook hands once more and Harm parted from the two sisters who were one with him in tribulation, one in faith, and soon to be one in the eternal joy of their Lord.

15

In the Cell and Before the Bailiff

A few moments later Harm Hiddesz found himself in a cell which, judging by the noise of passing wagons, must be several feet below street level. The door of the cell opened into a narrow corridor and while passing through it Harm counted three doors similar to the one he entered. A cross-barred opening in it served both to let in light and air and to hand food through it for the prisoners.

The jailer's servant who accompanied Harm, had lighted his lantern before descending the second stairway. When he opened the door of the cell assigned to Harm, such an unbearable stench met Harm that he automatically recoiled. But the bad air did not seem to bother the servant.

"You will get used to it," he said to his prisoner; "and it will get better after a few days. Only this morning we removed the last occupant."

"Was he sentenced to death?" Harm asked.

"No doubt he would have been in the end, had he lived long enough," the servant replied. "But he died yesterday morning, I believe. For a couple of days he had refused his food, but as you can imagine, we can't be bothered by people of his kind. Maybe he died even earlier," the servant added nonchalantly; "it is impossible to keep track of such things. When we discover it, that is soon enough for us.

"But come on, go inside! One would think that you are afraid of death! And heretics aren't scared of death, are they?" the man said, laughing scornfully.

"Look, there's fresh straw to lie on. The water crock is full. And early tomorrow morning I'll bring you your bread."

"Can I obtain a candle here, and writing material, and also a bed — for money, of course?" Harm asked.

"Not here!" was the reply. "Those sorts of things you do not need here very long anyway. I think that your case will soon come up, and no doubt they will reach a verdict in no time!"

In vain Harm tried to persuade the servant. The man departed and soon Harm was all alone in the dark cell — alone with his God.

He sat down on the wooden bench which was attached to the wall and gave free rein to his thoughts. A few days ago he had stood at the deathbed of his Adriaan. Should he not thank God that He had taken the boy to be with Him, for what would it have done to the lad if he had had to share this miserable place with his father? Harm wondered what the people had done with the child's body. No doubt his son had been buried in the corner where the suicides and condemned were buried. What else would they have done with the son of a heretic! But what of it! The Almighty Savior would also awaken the body of the lad and resurrect it to life eternal on the last day. It was a great comfort to him that he had been allowed to witness the departure of his son and that he had the assurance that his child had gone on before him into glory.

Harm Hiddesz knelt down and prayed. In the dark cell he experienced the communion of the Holy Spirit and, like David of old, strengthened himself in the Lord his God. Without realizing it he prayed louder and louder until his prayer became a psalm of praise. To be accounted worthy to suffer for the name of his Savior became a great privilege to him in that hour, for which he humbly thanked the Lord; and when he concluded his prayer by crying, "Amen! Amen! Even so, come quickly, Lord!" a voice in the dark corridor answered, "Amen, Amen!"

Was this an echo that repeated Harm's words? The prisoner had not noticed an echo before.

He wrapped himself in his mantle and lay down on the straw, on the very spot where a few hours before another martyr had died, one whose name, like those of so many thousands, had escaped the annals of history but which were written down in the book of life in heaven.

It was very quiet. Every now and then Harm thought he heard the lapping of water against the outside walls. He wondered if his cell bordered on the IJ.

In vain Harm tried to get to sleep. The emotions of the past few days left him no peace. Suddenly, however, he jumped up. He had unmistakably felt something crawl over him. There was no doubt about it! His cell bordered on the IJ River, and the water rats had free access to his room. Harm was very courageous in every other respect, but he simply loathed these creatures. The thought that they ran over his body filled him with horror.

Again he lay down on the straw and listened if he still heard the horrible creatures. It remained quiet for a while. Then he heard scratching again and at the same time something cold swept across his face.

Harm could stand it no longer. Again he got up and tore a strip of cloth from the lining of his mantle. With his tinderbox, which he always carried with him, he made fire and got the strip glowing. On the stone floor of his cell he arranged some straw from the pile, placed the burning cloth in the middle of it, and by constantly blowing caused it to catch fire. Once the fire got going he got some more straw in order to find, by the light of the fire, the holes through which the vile animals came inside. But he had not expected that the smoke that poured from the damp straw had no way of escape except through the cross-barred window in the door.

Just in time, he discovered from his difficult breathing to what great danger he had exposed himself. He had no choice but to extinguish the fire and try to get some sleep sitting on the wooden bench.

After having thus spent a few hours during which he had shut his eyes a few times from utter exhaustion, he woke up,

In the Cell and Before the Bailiff

little relieved and even more tired than before. A faint glimmer behind the window came filtering into the corridor and told him that it was morning. He listened attentively to determine by the noise of the passing wagons outside in which part of the Holy Cross Tower he was, but because of the increasing number of moving vehicles he could not tell whether he had been imprisoned on the side of the IJ River or in the back part of the tower.

Then, suddenly, Harm heard a man's voice begin to sing the words of a well-known song:

> *The Lord is stronger than castle or tower;*
> *Protect me, Lord, in this dark hour*
> *From all my foes who hatred breathe.*
> *Thou art, oh Lord, my strength and power,*
> *Oh snatch me from the lion's teeth!*
> *Lord, none, in battle, are like Thee;*
> *Oh King, who sets Thy people free,*
> *I yearn, Lord, to appear before Thee.*
> *Oh save me from my misery*
> *And call me to Thy realm in glory!*

Harm Hiddesz was not surprised that more people were incarcerated in this place for their faith, but it gave him joy to be able to sing this song of affliction along with the singer, and so he sang at the top of his lungs.

When the song was finished, Harm knelt down and prayed long and earnestly. Comforted and encouraged, he arose, and as the light in the cell had become somewhat brighter, he again inspected the room in which he might have to spend several weeks.

While he was busy doing this, the jailer's helper came downstairs and brought him bread and a hot fluid. He also informed Harm that in a couple of hours he would have to appear before the bailiff for his first interrogation. Whatever questions or requests Harm uttered, however, the servant responded to none of them. But when Harm slipped a Zeeland half-crown into his hand through the open window, the man became more responsive, and promised that he would try to incline the jailer to make Harm's stay in the cell more bearable.

As the servant had said, a few hours later Harm was removed from his cell and, shackled, taken upstairs into a room where the bailiff, who was sitting all by himself at a table, began to question him.

Harm Hiddesz, however, taught by the experience of others, was very careful what he said, and spoke nothing but what he deemed necessary. By urgent reasoning he complained that he, a traveling merchant, had very recently, when returning from Flanders, been apprehended without being convicted of any guilt whatsoever, and so he requested to be brought before the tribunal of the city magistrates in order to hear the accusations brought in against him, and thus to evoke a verdict from them. Harm Hiddesz, who knew only too well that a hearing before the Inquisitor was equal to a death sentence, tried by appealing to the magistrates to escape this danger.

He also knew that the Amsterdam magistrates, generally speaking, were not as vehemently opposed to the principles of the Reformation as the itinerant inquisitors whom they, according to the proclamations, were supposed to support. Indeed, the city rulers of Amsterdam, before the revolt of the Anabaptists, had been favorably inclined toward the Reformation.

The bailiff, who wanted to finish the many pending cases as quickly as possible, promised Harm that he would soon send him before the magistrates who alone were authorized to pass judgment on the prisoner.

Sooner than Harm Hiddesz could have expected, he was again summoned from his cell one morning and taken before the bailiff and magistrates where the prisoner, according to the judicial procedure in those days, was granted the mediation of an advocate, a certain Cornelus Lievens.

The bailiff, as the prosecutor, demanded sentence in the following words:

"Harmen from Antwerp, or whatever your correct name may be, I charge you in the name of His Majesty, in his capacity as Duke of Holland, and in my own, as Bailiff of Amsterdam, with having been rebaptized, which is contrary to the ordinance of the Holy Christian Church, and which is forbidden by His Majesty under penalty of forfeiture of life and possessions. I further charge you with having received into your house in Antwerp certain Lutherans who had been banished from the city on account of their Lutheran heresies,

In the Cell and Before the Bailiff

although it is forbidden by proclamation of His Majesty to do so under penalty of forfeiture of life and possessions. I conclude, therefore, that if I can convict you of these charges, or either one of them, that you will forfeit life and possessions, and that I shall carry out this sentence through the hangman until body and soul are separated."

The advocate, Cornelus Lievens, replied to this charge, "Lord bailiff, Harmen says that you are duty-bound first to give sufficient proof concerning this matter to the magistrates that is satisfactory to the presiding judge of this court, and that you must show why you have imprisoned him; and that he therefore should be acquitted of your sentence and his imprisonment."

The Bailiff replied, "I may apprehend a man without having prior proof, by virtue of my office! And since this Harmen is a foreign merchant and this trial has been assigned to me by others, I conclude therefore that I must have two weeks to gather proof."

Cornelus Lievens answered, "Lord bailiff, Harm says that you are obligated to justify your sentence to this tribunal, and that a prosecutor must at all times be ready to prove that his sentence is just. And since you have apprehended him without having proof of his guilt, he should be released at once."

The bailiff replied to this demand, "Since Harmen is an alien merchant, and since this matter took place outside the earldom of Holland, namely, in the city of Antwerp, in the duchy of Flanders, I ought therefore to have two weeks to gather proof or witnesses. So I demand that the magistrates pronounce sentence."

Cornelus Lievens countered, "Gentlemen, Harmen says that my lord the bailiff should not be given time to gather proof, but ought to have gathered all his proof before he apprehended him. He concludes therefore, as before, that he ought to be acquitted and released; and he demands trial by the magistrates."

The magistrates now charged with handling the case arose and, in the words of a historian, took "counsel together according to the custom of the city of Amsterdam. They summoned the bailiff and two magistrates, desiring to speak with them. And they asked him: 'Lord bailiff, what grounds do you have for your sentence?' To which the Bailiff answered, 'This

Harmen has been referred to me by letter from the Provincial Inquisitor of Utrecht as being guilty of belonging to the sect of the Anabaptists and of being polluted by Lutheranism, which Anabaptists he has regularly executed by fire and sword without informing the magistrates.'"

Furthermore, in answer to the demand by the advocate for proof, he said, "It was not my idea to postpone the sentence but I have been forced to do so on account of Harmen's request. Hence I conclude that I must have two weeks to gather my proof, as I have mentioned in my address."

The magistrates then took their seats and decided to grant the bailiff two weeks to gather information and to present his case anew, trusting that then they would be in a position to pronounce sentence, since they felt that now they were not able to handle the case fairly.

Harm Hiddesz was returned to his cell. His advocate, who had wanted to make use of the fact that the bailiff had no proof of Harm's guilt to obtain an acquittal from the magistrates, had lost his case insofar that the bailiff had been granted a postponement of two weeks in order to gather such proof. It was the fact that Harm Hiddesz had been imprisoned by Del Castro himself that made the magistrates declare "not to be in a position to pronounce sentence." Hence the chance that Harm might be released because of lack of proof was gone. And during the two weeks that had been granted the bailiff before Harm's next appearance before the court, much could take place to make his situation hopeless.

Harm, however, remained of good courage, and the conviction that the course of events had been so determined by God's counsel and by nothing else, strengthened him. "When soon I shall have to give an account of my faith," Harm thought, "my faithful God will sustain me and make my tongue ready to confess His Name and, if necessary, also to seal this testimony with my life."

With his head held high Harm left the courtroom, passing several prison guards near the door who had been listening in and who had been awaiting the verdict.

Suddenly Harm Hiddesz stopped. Among this small group of guards he noticed a deformed person who reminded him

In the Cell and Before the Bailiff

immediately of Bouke, Hannes's servant. And when he came closer to him, he was sure it was the man who in the hour of danger had so bravely defended him. The broad-shouldered man with the long arms also looked with his one eye at Harm, but so indifferently that the prisoner thought that he must have been mistaken on account of the remarkable similarity between this man and Bouke. After all, how could it be possible that Bouke was among these rough men who made fun by pushing the hunchback, amid gales of coarse laughter, from one to another? It was unthinkable, indeed, impossible that Bouke should be a keeper in the Holy Cross Tower, for had not the skull of the poor farmhand been crushed in the unequal fight with the Fleming? "Truly," Harm thought, "even if the earth gave back its dead, then it would certainly not do so in order to make Bouke a guard in the prison of those who are persecuted for the sake of their faith!"

But Harm had not been mistaken! It was indeed Bouke who stood there at the entrance of the courtroom, even though his scar-covered face did not show the emotion he felt upon seeing the prisoner again. But how had Hannes's servant gotten to this place?

As we remember, the blow which Antonio had dealt Bouke had knocked him out; but he soon recovered from it through the care of Hannes and Melis, and the wound rapidly closed, even if it did not heal quite as fast.

His friends had not been able to change his mind regarding his intention to go and search for the preacher and, if possible, to get in touch with him. It was as if an irresistible power drove Bouke to Harm, a power that was stronger than the fear of the dangers to which he inevitably exposed himself in doing so.

Armed with his heavy stick, to which he had attached a small bundle of clothes, he had started out for Leyden. Harm Hiddesz' Bible and a lock of Adriaan's hair were carefully hidden in his jerkin. When he learned in Leyden that the prisoner had been taken to Amsterdam, he immediately started out for that city, sometimes hiking a ride with some farmer, sometimes walking; and he finished the trip with such speed that he arrived in Amsterdam only one day after Harm Hiddesz.

As he had promised Mrs. Hannes before he left and upon her insistence, he went straight to a vegetable merchant, one of the many secret adherents of the Reformation who used to live in Leyden and was well-known to Hannes and his wife. When he had found him at last and not without considerable difficulty, these good people threw up their hands in amazement about the plan Bouke unfolded before them. They were of the opinion that only his utter ignorance concerning the many dangers to which he would be exposing himself had moved the servant to such an undertaking. They further told him so many gruesome stories about the persecutors and the executions that anybody except the stubborn Bouke would have abandoned his plan to venture into the lion's den.

Normally there would have been no objections to visiting prisoners; in fact, it was even permissible to take them food and small treats. The fear, however, to be considered a fellow heretic and to be spied upon by secret agents of the Inquisition kept many people from visiting the prison of heretics.

Regardless what these people told Bouke, however, he remained deaf to their warnings. As a precautionary measure he entrusted Harm Hiddesz' Bible to the keeping of the vegetable merchant and started out for the Holy Cross Tower.

The merchant, who accompanied him until they came close to the prison, now turned back. Shaking his head, he looked once more at Bouke who briskly walked toward the prison.

There stood Bouke, in front of the monstrous stone structure. On the way he had wondered a thousand times how he would ever be able to enter it; still he had not figured out a way. To ask for Harm Hiddesz and to request to be allowed to visit him he thought too risky; nor would this serve his purpose. But in what other way could he find entrance?

There he stood in the afternoon in front of the guardhouse — in which a few soldiers sat around — undecided and hesitant. He looked around; finally, he wondered if he ever would get inside.

"Lord," Bouke whispered, "Thou knowest that I have a message for Thy servant who is sighing in there in bondage for Thy Name's sake; wilt Thou help me now to carry out my task!"

In the Cell and Before the Bailiff

Suddenly Bouke got an idea when he saw the pewter mugs standing on the table in the guardhouse. Boldly he walked into the room, sat down on the wooden bench, put his stick and bundle on the table and, picking up an empty beer mug, pounded it on the table as if he were in a tavern.

The three soldiers first looked at each other and then at Bouke, and at last they burst out laughing.

"Well, your lordship, what is it you desire?" one of them asked mockingly, turning to Bouke.

"A pint of good beer and a place to sleep!" Bouke replied, and with his one eye he looked so stupidly at the man that the latter really thought he was dealing with someone who was not in his right mind.

"But where is the castellan?" Bouke asked, looking around.

"We shall get him for you in a minute," the soldier replied and turning to his friends, he said, "Let's play a joke on him!"

In the days of our story the man in charge of a castle or fortress was called a castellan, but so was an innkeeper, and so the man in charge of the Holy Cross Tower could be addressed by that name as well.

The soldier rang the big bell on the door through which Harm Hiddesz and the two women had entered and whispered something in the guard's ear. The latter left, laughing, and soon returned with the jailer.

"Here's the castellan," one of the soldiers snapped at Bouke.

"What do you want?" the jailer asked in surprise, turning to Bouke.

The farmhand looked from the jailer to the laughing soldiers like someone who had just discovered that he had made a mistake.

"Oh, excuse me, sir!" Bouke said bashfully, and bared his head, nervously fumbling with the hat in his hands. "I thought that this was an inn when I saw these mugs on the table and the doors open, and that's why I asked for the castellan. But I can tell that you are no innkeeper!"

"What's the meaning of this misplaced joke?" the jailer asked, annoyed, turning to the guard and the soldiers. "Do you know, little peasant, where you are? Do you know what kind of an inn this is?"

Bouke shrugged his shoulders.

"This place is an inn where it is best never to enter as a guest, because the chances of ever getting out again are little indeed! This is the tower in which heretics and similar criminals are locked up!"

Startled, Bouke reached for his stick and bundle as if to leave in a hurry.

"Take it easy!" the jailer said, now also laughing on account of Bouke's hasty and awkward movements. "You don't have to run off like that! Tell me, where do you come from, and what are you doing here in town?"

"I used to live with a farmer near Leyden," Bouke answered, "and I have been told that here in Amsterdam I can find work and that the pay is good."

"And where do you think you will find work?"

"That I don't know," Bouke said.

"Have you ever seen such a dumb goose in your life!" the jailer cried. Then he was quiet as if he were thinking about something. "Are you strong?" he asked Bouke after a while.

The farmhand smiled, which made his face even uglier instead of more attractive. He then picked up one of the pewter mugs and crushed it in one hand as if it were paper.

"I don't mean it that way!" the jailer cried. "Anyway, I see, fellow, that you have a couple of strong hands on your body, and I can use someone like that. Do you want to come into my service?"

Bouke acted as if the idea to work in a jail horrified him. To the jailer this was all the more reason to urge him to stay, and the reader can well imagine that Bouke needed little coaxing. From that moment on Hannes's servant ate in company of the prison guards and slept in a small room above the entrance of the building. He did all the heavy work for which his enormous muscle power was needed.

Again two days passed which Harm spent all alone in daily communion with his God. How he wished he could get in contact with the other prisoners who, like him, suffered for the truth's sake, and who languished in bonds only a short distance away from him. But the heavy stone walls prevented any conversation, and a word spoken through the cross-barred window in the door reached the adjoining cell so imperfectly, and resounded to such an extent through the vaulted corridor, that it was impossible to speak with one another. Only the singing of the prisoners frequently broke the painful silence, and by means of the psalms that were sung one heart spoke to another in the holy communion of suffering, comfort, and hope.

During the hours of lonely contemplation, now no longer disturbed by rats, as Harm had pried some stones loose from the center of his cell and placed these in front of the holes through which the uninvited guests entered, the prisoner constantly recalled the promise, the fulfillment of which he formerly never doubted — the promise that he would meet his eldest son some day. Even during the night, when lying on the hard floor made sleeping impossible for him, he reflected on this promise and doubt arose in his heart whether he might have appropriated this promise out of a carnal desire. Does it not often happen, he asked himself, that a wish, constantly cherished by the flesh, in the end takes on the form of a promise which is believed to have been received in a special way from the Lord? And even if he did not deceive himself, should he not then much rather believe while he was still here on earth that he would meet his son in heaven when soon he would be summoned to finish his earthly life as a martyr? Would God's promise be less wonderful that way? Would its fulfillment then be less glorious for the father who feared the Lord? Oh, when Harm thought about seeing his wife and children again; when he reflected upon the blessed, never-ending fellowship which they would enjoy before the throne of God and of the Lamb, then his reins longed within him and with Paul he wished to depart in order to meet, albeit through the flames of the stake, his Redeemer! In such hours Harm Hiddesz became humble before God; he then felt unworthy to ascend the stake; he then discovered by the illumination of God's Spirit so many sinful and carnal desires within himself that he was constantly compelled to kneel down before God. He realized that still many ties, whose existence he had never suspected, bound him to this earth.

On the morning of the sixth day of his stay at the Holy Cross Tower, the prisoner noticed by the commotion and the opening and shutting of doors that something unusual was going on. Earlier than otherwise his guard came to give him his coarse bread, accompanied by Bouke who hastily swept Harm's cell with a broom. Again the similarity between this man and the farmhand of his faithful friends on the Vliet struck Harm. While he stood there, musing about that, the regular guard left to open the cell of another prisoner. Bouke made use of that opportunity. He quickly stepped over to Harm Hiddesz and whispered in his ear: "Keep courage, master! Trust in the promise of God that He will neither leave you nor forsake you!"

In the Cell and Before the Bailiff

Before Harm had recovered from his astonishment, Bouke shut the door of the cell with a bang and bolted it on the other side. Then the big key turned with a harsh sound in the lock, and the prisoner was alone again.

Harm did not know whether he was awake or dreaming. What was the meaning of Bouke's words, and how did he get here? Certainly, the Lord would not forsake or leave him. He would impart His nearness to His faithful followers even unto the stake; yet, these whispered words seemed to have a special meaning.

An hour before noon a group of several persons descended the stairs that led to the corridor flanking Harm's cell.

It was Del Castro, the Provincial Inquisitor who, headed by the jailer and the wardens and accompanied by the bailiff and some magistrates, came to investigate the situation in the prison personally.

When they were in front of Harm's cell, the jailer stopped and very politely said to Del Castro, "Your lordship, in this cell is locked up the prisoner who was brought here last week from Leyden."

"Open the door!" Del Castro replied in a commanding tone of voice. Harm's wardens opened the cell and Del Castro looked piercingly and sternly at the prisoner.

"Are you the Flemish merchant who was apprehended near Leyden?"

Harm Hiddesz nodded.

"Have you requested sentence from the magistrates?"

"That I have, sir," Harm replied, "because I am of the opinion that it is contrary to all customs to keep a person in jail without a sentence. I have been accused by the lord bailiff to be an Anabaptist, which is contrary to the truth and cannot be proven by the bailiff."

"I have asked for two weeks' respite," the bailiff now said to Del Castro, "to gather proof that this man is indeed polluted with Lutheranism and other heresies."

"This proof I shall give you tomorrow," Del Castro said. "A longer respite is not needed for him."

On their way out Del Castro said to the bailiff, "I had expected to find a peasant or an agitated scatterbrain like there are so many in these lands, but this one I consider far more dangerous. Lately, followers of Calvin are beginning to come here from the Flemish regions. They do not intend a complete overthrow of society as did the Anabaptists of Munster; they do not run around naked; they cause no disturbances nor revolt against the king; but they go further and touch the root of our most holy faith. They deliberately undermine the foundations on which our entire Holy Church rests, and so these people are the worst of all. Tomorrow I will personally begin his examination, and so I request you to have his documents ready by that time."

The bailiff bowed courteously.

The jailer was ordered to prepare the chamber of examination.

That afternoon, Harm Hiddesz received, besides his usual dish of yellow peas, a piece of fried meat and half a bottle of wine. He did not know that such a meal was given only to prisoners who had to undergo "sharp examination" (on the rack).

The next morning Del Castro, more serious than otherwise, entered the room where Cornelio, his secretary, was already working.

"You will have a hard day, my son!" Del Castro said, "and so you will have to show what you can do. Most likely the scene which you will witness will greatly affect your already tender disposition and weak nerves; but one soon gets used to these things, and besides, this is a thing the clerk of the Inquisitor must be immune to."

Cornelio looked at Del Castro, puzzled. The secretary's face was paler than usual. He looked sad, and it was evident that the dinner discussion at the house of the priest of St. Jacob's was still vividly on his mind.

"I want you to come with me and be present at a hearing of the heretic who was caught very recently. You write fast, and it is very important that his confessions will be recorded as completely as possible, so that he can be judged on their basis," the Inquisitor said.

A few hours afterwards Harm Hiddesz was taken out of his cell and told that he had to appear before the Inquisitor. The prisoner, who had anticipated this, was wholly prepared and let his hands be cuffed on his back.

In the Cell and Before the Bailiff

"Lord," he whispered softly, "Thy will be done. Make Thy servant faithful, faithful unto death. Give him words of a sound mind; open his mouth to resist the lie, and to magnify Thy Name."

Still praying, Harm Hiddesz proceeded. At the end of the corridor Bouke joined the man who led Harm. The two men seemed to have become the most intimate of friends.

After the prisoner had ascended the first stairway and started to climb the second one which led to the room where he had appeared before the magistrates, his guard indicated that they had already reached their destination. A door was opened and a large hall illuminated by a lantern and a few candelabra presented itself before his eyes. For a second he shrank back from it, but then entered the room with steadfast step. The cross-vaulted ceiling told him that this room was still below ground level; and once inside, the jailer could have assured him that no sound, no scream of pain, no matter how penetrating, would be heard outside. The large wooden bench with the windlass beside it, the big square pillar with the iron bands, and the many instruments of torture on the wall clearly told Harm that he was in the torture room where already so many before him had spent hours of unspeakable agony.

Around a table were seated Del Castro with the bailiff and a few magistrates who were to assist them in the interrogation. Several documents lay in front of Del Castro and a large hourglass stood beside the inkwell.

Cornelio was seated at the end of the table. When the prisoner entered, he looked up curiously. But what emotions overwhelmed the secretary! In that pale face, framed in a black beard, he thought he recognized features that carried him back many long years. Indeed, it seemed that he noticed the same emotions in the prisoner, for uninterruptedly the latter fixed his staring gaze upon the young man.

"Harmen of Antwerp, or whatever your real name may be," Del Castro said to the prisoner who had approached the table with his guards.

Cornelio was startled when he heard the name "Harmen." Harmen — that was the name of his father! But his father was from The Hague, and this prisoner did not contest the mention of Antwerp.

Cornelio succeeded in pulling himself together and with rapid pen wrote down the questions Del Castro asked the prisoner.

The Inquisitor at once concentrated his examination on matters relating to the Church and its beliefs. After having asked the prisoner when he had been to confession last, and when he had last observed a holy day — questions which Harm answered frankly — Del Castro asked whether he believed in the seven sacraments of the Holy Church.

Harm answered this question in the negative. He recognized only two sacraments, holy baptism and the Holy Supper.

"Are you an Anabaptist, then?" Del Castro asked.

Harm said that he believed in infant baptism.

"Are you a sacramentarian, then?" was the next question.

"If my lord means that a desecrator of the sacrament of the altar is called a sacramentarian, then I declare that I am wholly innocent. Do you mean, however, that a sacramentarian is one who denies the miracle in the mass, then, indeed, I am a sacramentarian. For I believe that the mass is an idolatry accursed of God; and I believe that your priests and monks are sacramentarians when they put a piece of bread, like that which the bakers display in their windows, on the tongue of the people and tell them that this is the real body of Christ."

Harm wanted to continue, but Del Castro ordered him to keep silence.

"You heard, gentlemen, and you, lord bailiff, how the heretic speaks of the venerable sacrament of the altar," Del Castro said, and his voice trembled with indignation, "the great, holy mystery he calls an idolatry accursed of God!"

"Do you need more proof to be convinced what a dangerous person we are dealing with? In the case of a simple wandering sheep of the Church I would be willing to attempt to convince him of his error by reasoning with him. In the case of this fellow, however, that would be casting pearls before swine. This heretic has, according to all kinds of information I have in my possession, not only attended conventicles, but has also led them as an ordained preacher."

"You don't deny that?" Del Castro said, turning to Harm Hiddesz.

In the Cell and Before the Bailiff

"That is true, sir. With the laying on of hands I have been sent out from Wesel and have, as the servant of Christ, preached the pure gospel to the poor flock whom you and your monks with your statues and pater nosters have barred from the way of salvation."

"And have you not also sold and distributed heretical and forbidden books?"

"That is also true. And, thanks be to God, I have already distributed so many Bibles that your whole Inquisition will not be able to destroy the seed that I, at God's command, have sown in these regions."

"I must admit," Del Castro said, "that I seldom come across so much impertinence! Do you realize that every word you say here is equal to a sentence of death that you pronounce upon yourself? Are you not acquainted with the placards?"

"Oh, yes!" Harm replied. "If I had not been acquainted with them, then surely the smoking stakes in Flanders and Holland would have informed me how the Roman Church wants to exterminate the faithful followers of God's Word. As for me, I am ready to offer my body as a sacrifice, and I fear, thanks be to God, neither your threats nor the stake; but as for you, you had better fear Him who can destroy both body and soul in hell!"

"Where have you held conventicles, or to whom have you given those books?"

"Would I also deliver my brother into your hands? Far be it from me!"

Del Castro looked at the persons seated with him at the table.

"I request the bailiff," he said, "to make preparations for a sharp examination, and I suggest to place this braggart under the drip for six pater nosters" (the time needed to recite the Lord's Prayer six times). The gentlemen nodded in agreement.

At a signal from Del Castro a man was admitted into the room whose head and the upper part of his body were covered with a white bag, with peepholes on the places where his eyes were.

Harm Hiddesz turned pale. Of all the kinds of sharp examination the drip was by far the easiest, but also the most terrifying one.

The prisoner was placed against the big vertical pillar in the center of the room. One iron band was fastened around his waist and another one around his neck so that he was tightly secured to the beam.

"So you do not want to mention any names?" Del Castro cried once more.

"I may not, I cannot! Oh God, stand by me!"

Del Castro gave a signal and turned the hourglass upside down. Then the first drop of water fell from the ceiling on the head of the martyr. He hardly noticed it. The second one fell and penetrated through his hair. And regularly, slowly, and uninterruptedly, like the pendulum of an old clock, the drop continued to fall, ever and ever on the same spot of Harm's head.

He steadfastly refused to answer the continuously returning questions, and with a powerful voice he started to sing:

Behold my agony, oh Lord!
In my affliction strength afford,
Lest I succumb and soon deny Thee.
Oh, keep me faithful to Thy Word
Until the bitter end if need be!

In the Cell and Before the Bailiff 139

A great emotion overwhelmed Cornelio. Was that not the song his mother used to sing? Were they not the very words which for days had rung in his ears when he thought about his parents? And did these words have to be repeated here in this torture chamber by that man whose look already had touched the very depths of his soul? The young man, who witnessed a sharp examination for the first time in his life, had the feeling that he was going to black out. Staggering, he arose.

Del Castro saw it while turning the hourglass over for the second time.

"Are you not feeling well, my son?" he asked.

One of the magistrates arose and led Cornelio out of the room. When Cornelio reached the door, he turned his head once more to the man at the pillar. Harm's eyes had followed the young man. In the features of the secretary of the Inquisitor he had recognized the image of his now blessed wife.

"Could it be possible?" Harm asked himself. "Lord, wouldest Thou fulfill Thy promise in this manner? My Hidde, my son, sitting beside my tormentors! Lord, then I could exclaim with Thy servant Job: 'Ah, that I had never been born!...'"

And the drip continued to fall on and on.

Once more Del Castro urged Harm Hiddesz to confess, but he received no answer.

For the third time the hourglass was turned over. Then the drip became unbearable. It was no longer drops of water that fell down — they were sledgehammers that threatened to split the head of the tortured man. His eyes became more and more cloudy. It seemed as if he heard all kinds of noises, the rumbling of wagon wheels, the rolling of thunder. In vain he tried to collect his thoughts; in vain he tried to arrange words into a prayer. Every time the small drop of water came down on his head with a terrible impact. For the fourth time the top half of the hourglass had run empty, and as calmly as the first time Del Castro turned it over.

The first raw scream reechoed through the vaulted room. Bouke, who had remained near the door, trembled over his entire body. He bit his lips until they bled and clenched his fists. But Bouke did not lose sight of the purpose for which he had come to Amsterdam.

With the utmost exertion he succeeded in controlling himself. He looked at Harm, who was enduring there the most terrible torture for the sake of Christ, and for the sake of the brethren! To save all those secret followers of the gospel who had sheltered Harm and who had sat with him at one table he had kept silence, and look how he now suffered!

With bloodshot eyes Harm tried with superhuman strength to free himself from the choking iron bands; he tried to evade that fatal dripping that would drive him insane if this torture would not stop soon. The Inquisitor turned the hourglass for the last time.

Then Del Castro arose, and in the same grave and curtly solemn tone of voice as before said to the bailiff and magistrates, "We shall continue the examination next week; right now we can't get anything out of the heretic anyway. But I assure you, gentlemen, that our interrogation will have better results next time. He will not forget the drip very soon."

"My secretary is not used to these scenes yet," he continued, turning with his companions to the door; and, speaking to the masked man, he ordered him to release the heretic from the beam.

In no time the iron bands were loosed and, staggering like a drunken man, the faithful servant of the gospel, still handcuffed, was taken to his cell by Bouke and the first guard.

When they arrived in the cell, Bouke wanted to take off the handcuffs while the prisoner with laboring breath and bulging eyes sank down on the wooden bench.

"What do you think you are doing?" the guard asked Bouke, greatly alarmed and stopping him. "Do you want this heretic to fly at you like a lunatic once he has his hands free? A person who has been under the drip is like a wild animal and liable to do anything!"

"Are you a man!" Bouke asked, laughing scornfully. "I am not afraid of two such heretics!" And to prove his great strength, he lifted Harm Hiddesz from the bench and laid him softly on the straw on the floor.

In the Cell and Before the Bailiff

"But this poor fellow may do harm to himself in his crazed condition," Bouke remarked, "and the Inquisitor would hold us responsible for that. If it is all right with you, I will stay half an hour with the heretic until he has calmed down a bit."

The guard eagerly accepted this suggestion and left Bouke alone with Harm.

"Master Harm!" Bouke whispered in the martyr's ear. "Master Harm!"

Harm Hiddesz looked into the farmhand's face. His memory returned slowly, and it seemed as if the sight of Bouke's deformed face made him feel good.

"He who perseveres until the end will be saved, isn't that right, master Harm?" Bouke whispered again.

The prisoner nodded. Then Bouke no longer hesitated to remove the handcuffs. He took Harm's head into his arm, stroked the wet, disarrayed hair straight and, knowing of no better way to calm the disturbed mind of the prisoner, Bouke recited all the texts from Holy Scripture that applied to Harm's condition that came to his mind.

"Have I been faithful, Bouke?" Harm asked, "and did I not betray anyone? I feel that in those vexing moments towards the end I was no longer myself."

"Rest assured, master," Bouke said, and pressed the hands of the suffering servant of the Lord.

For a while Harm lay still, his eyes closed. He moved his lips as if in silent prayer. Then he looked again at Bouke. "How did you get here, and what are you doing here?"

"I will tell you that later," Bouke replied. "When I come back later on tonight I'll bring your Bible along. Right now it is safely hidden in the straw of my mattress. And here you have," Bouke said, while retrieving a piece of paper from his jerkin, "a lock of Adriaan's hair."

With trembling fingers Harm accepted the paper, and with tears in his eyes he lifted the lock of hair to his lips.

"Faithful Bouke!" was all Harm could utter.

16

The Recognition

After a long sleep, which had almost completely restored and refreshed him, Harm Hiddesz awoke the next day. Only faintly some shimmering of light filtered through to his cell, but it was sufficient for him to see by. After having thanked God on his knees for His sustaining love, he got from underneath the straw of his sleeping place the Bible which had never left him during his greatest adversities; and it somehow seemed to him that there would come an end to his grievous afflictions. With joyful voice he commenced to read Psalm 46: "God is our refuge and strength, a very present help in trouble." The longer Harm read, the greater the joy in his soul became, and he cried out with the sacred poet of old: "The Lord of hosts is with us; the God of Jacob is our refuge. Selah!"

Again Harm heard footsteps and, although unwillingly, he hurriedly hid his book again underneath the straw.

It was Bouke who approached, accompanied by a young priest — the Inquisitor's secretary!

Harm Hiddesz recognized the clerk who had been present in the torture chamber the day before, and his heart started to beat wildly. Was it so unusual, then, that an imprisoned heretic was visited by monks and priests? On the contrary, Harm knew that those people often did everything they could to attempt to convince the heretics of their errors.

The Recognition

The secretary, too, seemed to hesitate to enter after Bouke had opened the door of the cell. At last he crossed the threshold, and asked Bouke to leave him alone with the prisoner. The servant retreated, but then stopped and stood listening in the hall.

"Master," the clerk began, "yesterday I was present at your interrogation and have written down your answers which so crushingly testify against you. Nevertheless, I have not come here to quarrel about differences of faith with you. There is another matter that has struck me when reading over your confessions once more, and which has made me wonder whether you are the person whom the people here think you are. So would you kindly answer quite unreservedly and openly a few questions that may be of the highest importance, possibly to you as well as to me?"

"I can hardly promise that in advance. But ask, sir; maybe I shall be able to answer you."

"You are being called Harmen of Antwerp. Were you born in that city?"

"It is true that I recently came from Antwerp, and I often stay there," was the reply, "but my place of birth is The Hague."

The clerk started to tremble.

"Have you," he continued, "known a cheese merchant in the Achterom by the name of Hidde?"

"That was my father," Harm said; "but why these questions?"

"Did you have a son who...."

Suddenly it was as if the scales fell from the prisoner's eyes.

"Hidde, my son!" Harm cried passionately.

"Father! Father!"—and the clerk threw himself at the bosom of the heretic and kissed the face of the prisoner. "Father, must I find you back in this place?"

Bouke stepped closer to the door and looked through the cross-barred window, greatly moved. "Found at last," he said to himself, "but, ah, Lord, under what circumstances!"

After the first emotions of the father and son had passed, each had to tell the other what had happened during the twelve years they had been separated from each other.

Harm told about his fruitless efforts to find his son; and Cornelio, now Hidde again, could fathom the deep grief that had tormented his father all these years.

Hidde then told what he knew about his mother's passing away. Undoubtedly the priest of St. Mary's Chapel in The Hague could not have imagined that his description of the deathbed of Harm's wife would be of such great importance and comfort to the imprisoned heretic. When Harm heard how his wife had passed away, singing for joy in the "peace through the blood of the cross," he knelt down and thanked God with a psalm of praise for the certainty that was now given him that his faithful wife had preceded him to the New Jerusalem on high.

Harm Hiddesz' prayer did stir Hidde's soul, but at the same time it made him realize what a distance separated him from his father.

The shocked secretary of the Inquisitor faced the cold reality. With all the urgency of his fiery, loving heart, he tried to move his father to return to the Holy Mother Church. How could he ever witness his father's execution? He exerted every ounce of power of conviction he possessed to save and keep his father, whom he had found back so unexpectedly. At his plea Del Castro would certainly pardon the heretic if he would return from the errors of his way.

Harm Hiddesz listened to his son. With great inner joy he listened to that voice which he had not heard for so many years; but his heart remained deaf to Hidde's arguments.

"Father dear!" Hidde cried at last, "answer me! Say that you will recant, and even if I had to go to the governess, I shall save you from the hangman!"

Harm Hiddesz smiled.

"Sit down beside me, Hidde," he said. "I have a message for you. This message will at the same time be the answer to your questions."

Hidde sat down beside his father, and Harm began, slowly and with great feeling, to describe the deathbed of Adriaan; and all the while he was speaking he unfolded the doctrine of justification, based on the eternal truth of God's free grace, to his son.

With an urgency of conviction as he had never felt before when preaching to an assembled crowd, Harm spoke to his son. And when he had come to the end of his story, and got the Bible from underneath the straw — the Bible Harm had

The Recognition 145

bought for Hidde's mother — he took from it the lock of Adriaan's hair and when Harm handed this lock to his son and quoted the words: "Tell my brother Hidde that I count on it to meet him in the City on high with the golden streets" — then the clerk burst out in bitter lamentations.

"I cannot, I cannot go along with you!"

"With my God all things are possible!" Harm Hiddesz exclaimed.

With a burdened heart Hidde took leave from his father and promised that he would soon come again.

That day and all night Harm Hiddesz spent in prayer. No food passed his lips. His prayer was one continuous wrestling with God, one continuous pleading on His promise. "I will not let Thee go, oh Lord God, until Thou hast blessed me, until

Thou hast given me my child back again also spiritually. Oh mighty God of Jacob, break the chains and fetters that bind my Hidde to error and superstition. Descend with Thy Holy Spirit into his heart. Set him free, Lord God Almighty, as Thou hast set me free!" Locked behind bars and with the prospect of death at the stake, Harm Hiddesz boasted of his freedom!

While the imprisoned servant of the gospel wrestled on his knees in prayer that night, the Inquisitor's secretary paced the floor of his bedroom, greatly disturbed. How could he lie down on soft down while his father had to sleep on straw in a damp, cold cell?

In the stillness of the night, broken only now and then by the monotonous cry of the night-watchman, he again and again heard the prayer of his father and saw in his mind the young lad, on his deathbed, whom he had known only as an innocent infant in a cradle.

Indeed, it was not a bad dream that vexed him, for the lock of hair, which his dying brother had assigned to him, lay there in front of him before the crucifix on the table.

According to the teaching of his church, this brother, as well as his mother, had died in heresy, and both were a prey of Satan and his demons. And soon he would have to behold his father being again taken before the court of religious inquiry, and he would have to witness the most cruel tortures which they undoubtedly would inflict upon him. It seemed as if he again heard the suspected heretic unfold before him the doctrine of justification. A terrible conflict raged in Hidde's soul. Had not Del Castro only recently reminded him of the words of Holy Scripture, "He who loves his father or mother more than me is not worthy of me"? What were all the sorrows of the past years compared with the fears that now gripped his heart?

He realized that he had to make a definite choice; either he must choose in favor of the church, and consequently follow her orders and be a persecutor of simple souls, but at the same time become guilty of the blood of his own father, or he had to choose in favor of his father. But that meant that he would be forever outside the church, along with all heretics, and facing eternal damnation.

The Recognition

These were moments of great anxiety for the clerk. He fell on his knees before the statue of Mary that stood in the corner of the room on a sort of pedestal. In vain he besought Our Lady and all the saints to show him the light in this grievous hour, if necessary even by way of a miracle, a supernatural apparition, or something of that kind, to deliver him from his doubts and to show him the way he had to go.

At the same time a prayer was sent up in the prison cell, but not before a statue of Mary bathing in the light of candles, but before the throne of grace, with a pleading on God's promise, "My spirit that is upon thee, and my words which I have put in thy mouth, shall not depart out of thy mouth, nor out of the mouth of thy seed, nor out of the mouth of thy seed's seed, saith the Lord, from henceforth and for ever." And the eternally faithful God to whom Harm Hiddesz prayed did not turn a deaf ear to his pleas. God was not a man that He should lie, nor a son of man that He should repent of anything. The Lord would gloriously fulfill His covenant promise on which His servant pleaded.

Although Hidde was not yet added to the flock of Christ that very night, nevertheless his name had been written from eternity in the book of life, and the Lord had reserved for him a new name which he, engraved upon a white stone, would receive out of the hand of God.

When morning dawned, Hidde had made his decision. He would do everything possible to get his father out of the country and across the border to safety; and even though by so doing he denied his calling and became unfaithful to the vows which he had made in the Roman church, that could not be helped. He would afterwards, when once they were in a foreign country where he was unknown, enter a monastery and do penance for the rest of his life. This was Hidde's decision.

The entire morning the clerk was working in the presence of Del Castro on the papers that would be used against his father, all the while contemplating on ways and means to free his father from prison.

When the Inquisitor left in the afternoon to pay separate visits to the bailiff and the magistrates, Hidde hurried over to the Holy Cross Tower. The soldiers of the guard arose respectfully when the young priest, the secretary of the Inquisitor, approached the gate. The jailer opened every door with the readiness and humility which he showed to any member of the "Holy Court."

Bouke, whom the clerk had beckoned, again led him to the cell of his father, who had already been waiting for him a long time. After a fervent embrace Hidde told about the battle he had fought that night and about his plan to run away, if possible, with his father.

"How can I run away and endanger your life and that of others?" Harm Hiddesz asked. "I am ready to give my life, if the Lord so demands!"

"I believe that you allow yourself to be carried away by your enthusiasm, Father," Hidde replied. "If a way of escape can be found, I believe that you must accept it. You have, according to your convictions, a holy calling; well then, why should you abandon that calling? Or would you rather see that I stayed in the service of the Inquisition? As far as I am concerned, I shudder from all those tortures and I do not wish to pollute my hands with others' blood, not even that of heretics. I shall travel with you; I shall take care of papers that will open a way across the border, and after that, well, then we can talk again and maybe each can go his own way."

Harm Hiddesz sighed. He might not reject Hidde's proposition. He already anticipated that he could bring his son into a different environment, under the influence of the gospel; so he accepted Hidde's plan.

The great difficulty was, however, how to get unnoticed through all those guards. For some minutes the two men pondered silently on this problem. Then suddenly Bouke appeared, who had heard the conversation between father and son from beginning to end.

Hidde was startled, but his father put him at ease and then informed him who Bouke was.

"With the Lord's help I will get you out of the tower," the farmhand said, and he told them a plan of escape which he had carefully considered and for which he had already made preparations several days before.

The Recognition

Bouke showed them two brand new keys. Since he carried the key to Harm's cell, he had made an impression of it in wax and had the blacksmith make a copy of it. Even though he had to turn in the regular key to the jailer after Harm's visitor had left, he could now unlock the cell of the prisoner any time he wished.

"And what about the other key?" Hidde asked.

"That one is to take us outside," Bouke answered. "At the end of the corridor, where the torture chamber is, there is a small door. After we descend a few stone steps, that door leads to the water which flows underneath a big cement arch to the River IJ. Underneath that arch, unseen by pedestrians above, is the boat in which many heretical women, bound in sacks, have been taken to the middle of the IJ at night to be thrown into the water."

Hidde shuddered at the thought of such cruelty.

"I have also made an impression of the key to that door, and the key patterned from it fits perfectly. So when your son Hidde takes care of the necessary papers, there is only one difficulty left."

"What is that?" Hidde asked.

"How do we get the money for the journey?"

"That is no objection!" Harm exclaimed. "My mantle does not only serve as a protection from the cold, it is also a safe hiding place for my money. In the collar of my mantle I sewed several gold pieces to use in time of need, and it was mainly for this reason that I sent for this piece of clothing from Hannes's."

The three men now decided that they should not wait long to carry out their plan, and it was agreed that they should try to venture the undertaking that same evening.

After discussing some further details, Harm Hiddesz and Bouke knelt down, and even Hidde, gripped by the seriousness of the moment, knelt with them. After a fervent prayer, in which Harm besought God for His help and support, Hidde left the cell in order to start immediately with his work at home.

Del Castro had not returned yet. Filled with apprehension, Hidde hurriedly prepared a number of seals with the imprint of the Provincial Inquisitor, and attached them to an equal number of parchments. After that he went to his bedroom and wrote the documents exactly in the form of the safe-conducts of that time.

At about eleven o'clock, at which time the streets of Amsterdam were completely empty, he carefully went outside. Instead of his long priestly robe, he now wore a short jerkin he had been able to secure.

When he reached the River IJ, he kept his eye on the dark passage from which, according to the plan, the boat was to appear, carrying his father and Bouke.

He constantly stared at that one point. The bells had announced the hour at which the boat was to appear a long time ago already, and he worriedly wondered whether the plan had possibly failed.

But then he saw some movement. The boat approached. With one jump Hidde was sitting beside his father. "Where's Bouke?" he asked, seeing that his father was alone.

"Caught," Harm Hiddesz nervously answered. "Here, take an oar and hurry; hurry, if you cherish your life!"

What had happened?

Everything had gone well and according to plan until Harm Hiddesz and Bouke had reached the door that led to the water.

But Bouke, not quite familiar with all the precautions that were taken in the prison to prevent any escape, had not counted on the night rounds. He had just turned the key in the lock when two armed watchmen had appeared in the corridor.

Bouke had immediately seen the danger they were in. "Run! Run!" he had screamed at Harm Hiddesz.

"Not alone!" Harm had said in reply. "Run!" Bouke had repeated, pushing Harm down the stairway. "Think of your son!"

At the same time he had slammed the iron door shut behind Harm, clutched the key in his iron fist, and awaited determinedly the watchmen who had leaped at him. "Betrayer!" one had shouted, "give me that key!"

"Never, as long as I live!" Bouke had answered.

A fearful struggle had ensued in the corridor, which now had been completely dark, as Bouke had knocked the lantern out of the hand of one of the guards.

"The key, the key!" they had screamed. "The heretic is escaping."

But Bouke had held on to it.

Suddenly a scream had resounded that had reechoed to the farthest vaults.

One of the guards had thrust his short dagger to the hilt between the ribs of the unfortunate Bouke. Mortally wounded, Bouke had crashed to the floor.

"Saved! I thank Thee, oh my God! They are saved!" were his last words; and the faithful servant fell as a sacrificial lamb for the sake of the brethren.

17

Ten Years Later

Again we take our readers back to The Hague. Nicholas Del Castro had laid down his office of Provincial Inquisitor long ago and had been received as its first bishop by the city of Middelburg on the third day of January, 1563. But other inquisitors still persecuted, by fire and sword even more vehemently than he ever had done, the ever increasing number of the followers of the Reformation. For every person who was martyred dozens of others came in his or her place, and the blood of the martyrs again proved to be the fruitful seed of the Church.

In the house in the Achterom we already know so well, which was now inhabited by a certain Gerrit Willemsz, a wool merchant, two men, silent and very serious, were standing in the room where the wife of Harm Hiddesz had fought her last battle. One of them we would have recognized at once. He was the former cheese merchant himself, whose hair and beard had turned gray and whose face bore the imprints of many cares and deprivations. The second person we would not have recognized as readily. He was Hidde whose features and appearance had changed much since the moment we saw him last when he had escaped from Amsterdam. The years had given him a more rugged look; the hardships of the times had matured him into a robust man.

For the first time after more than twenty years of absence they were standing here together again in the room where

Maria, the Flemish woman, had departed, boasting of peace through the blood of the cross.

Gerrit Willemsz, a warm adherent to the new doctrine and a faithful believer, entered the room and invited the "brethren" to follow him to the big warehouse back of his house. There Harm Hiddesz and his son found a small crowd of faithful Christians who, in spite of the placards, had been courageous enough to gather here to search the Word of God and to participate in the sacraments.

They all looked with keen interest at the young man who accompanied Harm Hiddesz. They already knew his history. They already knew that the preacher had escaped from prison in Amsterdam, together with the secretary of the Inquisitor, and that they had faced much danger in doing so. They had heard about the struggle of the young priest before surrendering willingly and giving himself to the service of the Lord, whereupon he had been solemnly ordained to the office of minister by the laying on of hands at a church meeting in Wesel. Now they would hear from his own mouth — the mouth of him who once sat at the table in the torture chamber of the Inquisition — the pure gospel, and behold in him a manifestation of God's faithfulness.

The father opened the solemn gathering with prayer. In the same place where he used to labor hard to earn his daily bread, he now boasted of the riches that are in Christ Jesus.

He opened the old Bible, his inseparable treasure.

There could be no singing! The enemies were probably not far away, and it would be not only careless but also irresponsible to arouse the suspicion of neighbors and passersby.

Harm Hiddesz read Psalm 77, the song which David had composed when his soul had been afflicted with sorrow, but the mighty Jehovah had sent deliverance; and the gathering attentively followed every word the preacher said.

"I will remember the works of the Lord; surely I will remember Thy wonders of old."

Harm had a fertile subject, for he could testify of great wonders and deliverances in his life. Was he himself not a living proof of the faithfulness of God? Had he not more than once been snatched from certain death as by a miracle? And did not his son stand across from him, ready to take over Harm's task in Holland, while he himself was called to other places to labor in the vineyard of the Lord?

Briefly he recalled for this small congregation in The Hague the remarkable events that had reunited him and Hidde at this place, and in a fervent prayer he commended his son to the faithfulness of God and the love of the congregation.

Then Hidde arose. A flood of emotions overwhelmed his soul now that here, at the place where he had spent his early years and where his now-blessed mother had breathed her last, he appeared under such entirely different circumstances from those of a few years ago. He also thought of the young lad whose remains rested out there at Voorschoten, but whose soul sang praises with all those who had been bought with the blood of the Lamb.

The deathbed of the lad and the words he had spoken which Harm, upon Hidde's request, had repeated at least a hundred times, filled him with a holy longing for the City of God on high. In these days of oppression and persecution, of grief and fear, of blood and fire, his eye of faith beheld the New Jerusalem as John saw and described it in the twenty-first chapter of Revelation.

"There will be no more persecution and lamentation, no fear of stakes and scaffolds, but there will be eternal singing by those who, while on earth, walked their pathway of life weeping and sighing; the anthems will resound to the honor of Him who loved His people already from before the foundation of the world and who bought them with His precious blood.

"Faggots may smoke; the Inquisition may multiply its attempts to quench the light of the gospel ten times; still hundreds and thousands more martyrs may have to seal their faith in free grace with their blood, but nothing shall separate us from the love of Christ!"

With these words Hidde concluded his sermon. And when a few moments afterwards the congregation gathered around the communion table, Harm Hiddesz, the old tried open-air-preacher, received the signs and seals of the new covenant from the hands of the former *secretary of the Inquisitor.*